WHEN MOVIES WERE A DIME

by
Ardyce Habeger Samp

Foreword By
William J. Janklow

RUSHMORE
HOUSE
PUBLISHING

RUSHMORE HOUSE PUBLISHING
2002

Published by
Rushmore House Publishing
Sioux Falls, South Dakota 57101
800-456-1895

ISBN: 1-57579-249-4

Library of Congress
Control Number 2002093083

FIRST EDITION

Edited by:
Karen A. Samp
Margaret E. Mesmer
Julie A. Samp

Cover design by
Richard Gorsuch

Printed by Pine Hill Press, Sioux Falls, South Dakota
Manufactured in the United States of America

Dedication

It is with love and gratitude that I dedicate this book to my children: Rolly and Karen, Cyndy and Duayne, grandchildren and spouses: Mike and Julie, Matthew, Rebecca and Eric, Elizabeth, Tony and Jennifer, April and Daniel.

May my great grandchildren, Jacob and Maggie and future generations catch a glimpse of life as it was during my life growing up in South Dakota many years ago.

To my sisters, LaVonne and Eileen, their spouses and relatives who have listened to my many stories with good humor, thank you.

I also dedicate this book to my many friends who have been interested in my writing. To mention a very few of them: Arthur Matson, Audrey Johnson, Iona Vigness, and my neighbors and friends in the organizations of which I am a member.

I love you all!

Ardyce

Foreword
by William J. Janklow

When I was growing up in the '50s in the Midwest, we lived in a world recovering from the Great Depression, the dust bowl, and World War II; yet our parents held steadfast in their optimistic determination to build a better future. Tom Brokaw labeled this driving force, "The Greatest Generation," because they built the America that is the foundation of our world today. They invented the American Dream, and then they achieved it.

History records the struggles of families losing businesses and farms, loved ones killed or maimed during the War, and the challenges to rebuild a world "safe for democracy." Within all the statistics, often missed are the lives of the real people who got up every day, went to work, went to church on Sunday, and had simple and intrinsic goals—God, Family, Country.

Ardyce Samp has captured snapshots of the lighter side of life during the middle part of the Twentieth

Century as only a writer of 50 years could do. She turns the clock back for just a moment and allows us to listen in on the lives of people who grew up during the Depression and won World War II, and who enjoyed life as only those who recognize its fragility can.

This is Ardyce Samp's third book of short stories, which follows her regional bestseller, *When Coffee Was A Nickel* plus *Penny Candy Days*. Tens of thousands of readers have enjoyed her writings for which she has received numerous awards. As one who has worked to preserve the memories of a unique time in our history, Ardyce may well be remembered as the "Laura Ingles Wilder of the Mid-Twentieth Century."

But Ardyce Samp's most important work may not be her writing. Her stories have been an inspiration and encouragement to readers to share the good times of a great era with their families. Ardyce's stories have spawned a rebirth of family storytelling. And she has taken her passion for writing into our schools, encouraging young people to write and to chronicle their daily lives in a journal. She also urges them to talk to grandparents and great-grandparents to learn their family legacy while they still can.

When Movies Were a Dime will transport you to the days of newsreels and serials at the Crystal Theatre in my hometown of Flandreau, South Dakota, where the hot buttered popcorn still permeates the air.

Enjoy!

About the Author
Ardyce Habeger Samp

When Movies Were a Dime is the author's third book. It is a sequel to *When Coffee Was a Nickel* and *Penny Candy Days*. The author's intent is to share a slice of life during the years before television, the "Dirty 30's, WWII and post war" years.

Those were the days when small towns were the hub of family life. Neighbors and kinfolk were the treasures of the heart. People worked hard but also had fun in the "good old days" when they were growing up.

Ardyce began her writing career in 1948 when she wrote *On the Range,* the first recipe column for the "Sioux Falls Argus Leader" and other area newspapers for more than twenty years. She sold her first writing to "Better Homes and Gardens", October 1948. Through the years, several hundred of Ardyce's stories have been published in state and national magazines.

Some of her awards include:

Governor's Award,
"South Dakota Historian of the Year"
South Dakota Historical Society, 1997

"South Dakota Writer of the Year"
South Dakota Hall of Fame, 1997

"Woman of Achievement Award in Journalism"
General Federation of Women's Clubs, 1998

"Certificate of Commendation"
American Association of State and Local History, 2000

"Dakota History Conference Award"
Distinguished Contribution in Preservation of Cultural Heritage on the Northern Plains, 2000

Ardyce Samp was elected to the South Dakota State Historical Society Board (1998-2001) and is a Governor's Appointee for the South Dakota State Humanities Council (1998-present).

Table of Contents

A Cheap Date in '38

Oliver Patterson was a high school senior in the spring of 1938. He was anxious for graduation, as he had his plans for his future. He wanted to go to college in the fall. He would also enlist in the National Guard so he would have money for college tuition. He knew that all men age 18 were required to register for the draft for possible military service. He also knew that America might be involved in war. The Great Depression was ending. Jobs were available and farm prices were better, but he did NOT want to spend his life on a farm.

Oliver had not dated. His sisters and their friends were all he needed to know, he thought. He would save his money for a college education. He had worked hard the past three years helping his father on the farm replacing the hired man.

He shoveled snow for elderly people. Since money was scarce, he did not receive much for the work, as many felt young men should help them as a favor. Frankly, he hoarded every hard-earned dime.

Oliver's friends told him that he was missing a lot of fun by not dating girls, taking them to movies on Saturday nights or to dances at the area pavilions. He thought about it but wondered if it was really worth spending his hard-earned money.

During study hall at school in April, Oliver found himself staring at a sophomore girl, Greta, who was very popular with his friends. She had beautiful blonde hair and was always smiling. "She's smart, too!" he heard his friends say. Her name was Greta Thompson. He watched her as she studied and decided he would take a chance and ask her for a date. He could take her to a movie at the new Roxie Movie Theater and buy popcorn plus a Coca-Cola, all for a dollar. Movies were ten cents in the afternoon but a quarter at night. Oliver also had heard friends say that the new Hollywood shows cost fifty cents. He pondered on how to best ask Greta for a date. He decided to put a note in her desk during the noon hour. He wrote: "Would you go to a movie with me on Saturday night?" If she did not respond, it would be better than asking her in the hallway after school and be embarrassed by her rejection.

Greta found the note after lunch. As a response, she pretended to use the pencil sharpener, which was located on the wall across from Oliver's desk. She quickly dropped a paper on his desk. He rapidly put it in his pocket. When no one was looking, he took it out. The note was one word. "YES!"

With this response, he hoped that Dad would let him use the old Ford truck for his first real date. In addition to church on Sunday and for funerals, the family used their passenger car on Saturday nights to go to town to buy groceries, sell eggs and milk, as well as visit with their friends and neighbors. They met in the grocery stores, barbershop, drugstore and the pool hall to exchange stories heard during the week, and debate different views on everything from the weather to politics. But Oliver was not allowed to drive the car.

While Oliver was riding home on the bus, several of the girls were laughing and talking more than usual, as if they had a secret. When Oliver's sisters got off the bus, they ran up the driveway to tell their mother the news. "Oliver has a date with Greta on Saturday night!"

When Dad came in the door, his daughters were reciting the old time ditty, "One for the money, two for the show, three to get ready, four to go!"

Oliver did not think this was funny! Nevertheless, he headed out for chores thinking more and more about what his first date would really be like.

By morning, the news of the date had been discussed on the party telephone line. Everyone seemed happy to think that Oliver finally decided to date. And his choice was approved by all.

Following a brief talk on Friday's lunch hour. Greta got a note saying that Oliver would pick her up at 7:00 P.M. They would go to Webster City. Greta was to decide which movie they would see. The State Theater was showing *Boystown*, with actor Spencer Tracy. Since *Boystown* is located near Omaha, Nebraska, it would be a sure crowd pleaser. The Roxie Theater's movie was playing *Alexander's Rag Time Band*, one of the best movies of 1938. It would be a difficult choice to make.

"What movie will you see? Will you go to the Roxie or State Theater?" Mom and Dad asked at dinner. They were happy for Oliver to date Greta, as he usually worked and studied every night. They also reasoned that he wanted to join the military, as he thought there might be a war with Germany. "Nobody can predict the future at this time, so he deserves a few nights of fun."

When Oliver was leaving in the old Ford truck, his dad pressed a dollar bill into his hand. With the money Oliver had taken from his savings, it would be a very good date.

Greta was ready when Oliver stopped at her family farm for the date. Her father and mother stood at the

3

door and waved as they left. It was a message of satisfaction for the young couple and permission to have an enjoyable evening.

Oliver was driving along the gravel road toward Webster City and he smiled at Greta. The weather was wonderful and the excitement of the evening was just beginning.

Suddenly, there was a noise and then a big bump in the truck!

Oliver jammed his foot on the brakes. Both nearly hit the windshield. "FLAT TIRE!" he yelled, as he jumped out of the truck. "I've been telling Dad that we needed new tires on the truck. I don't have a spare! I'll have to walk as far as the paved road and wait for help!"

Before he could gather his thoughts, a truck came up behind them and stopped. "Flat tire, I see! I'll help you put on another one. I always carry an extra. We'll put this on and you'll be ready to roll." It was Howard Jerstad, a neighbor just down the road who lived next to Oliver's uncle's farm, coming to the rescue as neighbors always did for each other.

Greta sat in the truck feeling almost bruised by the jolt, but the real problems were the bugs! It was near sunset. The mosquitoes were just coming out and there were grasshoppers everywhere! It was too hot to roll the windows all the way up, so she swatted the bugs as best she could.

When the tire was changed and the truck started again, Oliver apologized for the flat tire. Greta told him that all was well and they would enjoy the movie. By the time they got to Webster City, found a parking place on the busy street, and walked to the theaters, they found people standing in a long line. An usher told them that all the seats were taken. If they wanted to wait for the 10:00 P.M. show they might be able to get a

seat then, he suggested. This was the case at both theaters.

Oliver and Greta went back to the truck and looked
at each other. "Now what?" they said, almost simultaneously. "I smell popcorn," Greta said, and "I'm
thirsty." The popcorn wagon was at the end of the
street and people were lined up to buy bags of hot buttered nickel popcorn. Since they were thirsty, they
decided to go into the Molly's Café across the street.
They each ordered a "fountain coke", which came in a
large glass with ice cubes in the bottom. There were
large paper straws in a glass container. They finished
their popcorn and drank the delicious beverage. "Life
is good," they both thought...movie or no movie.

Greta said, "Why don't we drive out to the dance
hall at Gordon's Beach? They always have a good
orchestra for their Saturday night dances." Oliver
thought a few minutes and then said, "Do you know I
can't dance?" Greta replied, "We can park outside and
listen to the music. Sometimes they let people in to
watch and listen. What do you think?"

"Good idea!!" was Oliver's response. Arriving at the
dance pavilion by the lake, they listened to the band
playing a new of kind of music called "the jitterbug." It
was the newest dance craze. They had fun listening to
the popular music and watching the dancers "jitterbug."

When the band began playing "Show Me the Way to
Go Home," the couple decided to leave before traffic
would become heavy and leave clouds of dust in the
air. The trip home was pleasant. The moon was bright
and stars filled the sky. The night had been a special
one, to both of them.

As they drove into Greta's family farmyard, there
was a bright gasoline light shining from the table in the
living room. Greta's dad came out to the truck and

asked why they were coming home so late. "Tomorrow is Sunday," he said, "and church starts at 9:00 A.M." Oliver got out, opened the door and helped Greta out of the truck. He said, "Good night," and Greta said, "Thanks!" There was no chance for a hug or kiss.

When Oliver got home, his father was waiting for him. The flat tire was the real concern for his dad, as they would now need to buy a new tire. But he was glad to hear Oliver had a good first date.

Oliver and Greta did not have another date. They both felt rather strange after their first date, as if it were too good to be true. Oliver graduated in May and was busy throughout the summer helping his father on the farm. In the fall, he joined the National Guard and enrolled at State College. He had a part-time job at college and with the National Guard drills, his busy life did not give him time for dating.

Greta was popular with the young men in her class, but none were like Oliver. She helped her parents on the family farm and did babysitting for neighbors, saving money for college. She planned to attend Eastern Normal College for one year; then she could teach grade school students in one-room country schools. Annually she would attend summer school so she could eventually teach in town schools.

After graduating in 1940, her wishes came true. She enrolled in college pursuing her teaching degree. But the world was rapidly changing. The boys were still dating girls when they had time, but most of them had joined the National Guard and were preparing for the possibility of the United States getting into a war.

In March 1941, the National Guard was called into action in anticipation of war. Then the Japanese bombed Pearl Harbor on December 7, 1941. The men who had not enlisted in the National Guard were drafted into the military. The girls finished their educa-

6

tion or took jobs in a world with little social life with young men.

Oliver and Greta lost touch with each other for over 40 years.

An Invitation...

In 1988, Oliver had retired from his government job and moved an hour from the family farm to a city called Bridgeport. The relatives had mostly died or moved away but it was still home. He often wondered what happened to his high school friends, including Greta Thompson.

When Oliver picked up his mail one morning, he wondered why his former high school class president would be writing him. He opened the letter basically out of curiosity. It was an invitation to attend an all-school reunion to be held on July 4th. It would be held in the new community building recently built in their small hometown. The school had been closed for 28 years due to low enrollment, but the reunion sounded great to Oliver. He hadn't seen his hometown friends in years.

When the 4th of July arrived, Oliver was excited, as he would be celebrating the 50th anniversary of his graduation class. There would be a parade at noon and a banquet in the evening. He was more excited about this event than anything in recent years.

He was assigned to ride in a horse-drawn wagon with members of his class during the parade. Oliver arrived early and met most of the members of his class of 1938. A few lived too far away to attend the reunion plus several were deceased. They all looked in awe of "what a difference 50 years makes!"

As he stood waiting for the parade to begin, he noticed a handsome woman standing beside him. He looked at her and she smiled as if she recognized him.

Almost simultaneously, he said, "Greta?" and she responded, "Oliver?"

The parade started as he jumped into the wagon, but to his own surprise, he told Greta, "Wait for me after the parade!" She nodded and then joined the crowd on Main Street. Oliver waved as the 50-year class wagon rolled past her.

He located her when the parade ended and suggested they go out to the city park for a visit. The lunch was being held there under the beautiful trees and among the flowers. This made a lovely place for alumni and families to visit before the evening programs.

By the time they reached the park, the food line was long. Oliver said, "If you aren't too hungry, let's wait in the car and visit a little." For a few minutes, both were silent. Then Greta asked, "Are you married?"

Oliver said, "No, I was never married! My job took me into foreign countries and into large cities all over America. I dated some, but none of them seemed to be what I wanted. I did hear that you were married. I guess I just never found a girl who really attracted me like you."

Greta thought a short time and then responded, "My husband died 19 years ago of a sudden heart attack. I have been a high school teacher for many years. I've raised two daughters who have good jobs and are married and they have given me four grandchildren. I retired last year and am living in my home here in Bridgeport where I plan to stay."

Oliver was quiet while he thought how to react to this news. He finally reached over to Greta and held her hand. Tears were running down her face. Oliver did not know if she was happy or sad.

"I've been living in Bridgeport, since I retired, but I had no idea you were in the same town!"

8

By this time, an old friend of Oliver's knocked on the window and told them they should eat before it was too late. They slowly got in line, and were happy to visit more as they sat across from each other.

Several people who joined them during their lunch interrupted their personal conversation. Friends recalled the years when the high school band won awards and when the basketball team won the state championship.

During the afternoon, the park dance pavilion was open for people to visit. Some alumni had relatives and friends in the area so they spent time with them. Oliver and Greta both had distant relatives in town to visit, so they quickly exchanged addresses and telephone numbers in case they were not together again that day.

The all school reunion brochure provided information that included a notice that each class would be eating together at the banquet, and that all should stay for pictures which would be taken immediately after the banquet.

Greta left immediately after her class picture was taken and headed home. She wanted to be with her family since it was the 4th of July, an annual tradition. Oliver told his class members that he was leaving after the picture was taken as he had business to attend.

When Greta arrived home, there was a note on her table from her family that they were all going to the city fireworks display and would be celebrating until late. They would come and spend the day with her tomorrow.

As soon as Oliver got to his home, he telephoned Greta. "I left the reunion because of business concerns. My important business was to see YOU," he said. "May I come over now? I think I can find your house if you leave on a front light! I can't be too far from your address."

"Okay," was Greta's reply. She then rushed to her front door and put on the light. Greta was so nervous with the change of events that she walked the floor waiting for Oliver to drive up and come to her door.

As soon as she heard a car stop in the driveway, she opened the door and Oliver came running to her. He grabbed her and hugged her. Then, to her surprise, he kissed her cheek! By this time, both were laughing and hugging!

They sat on the sofa in front of the TV, but they were not listening to the program. They began telling each other about their lives the past 50 years. Greta offered him a glass of wine. He said that he would enjoy some soda, but he didn't drink liquor or smoke. "I hope to live for many more years," was his comment, "and I hope you do, too!"

Greta told about her daughters, their husbands and jobs. Then she showed him pictures of her grandchildren. "Two of them are engaged to be married this fall." she told him.

After both ran out of things to talk about from their past, they sat silently on the sofa. It was midnight and the 4th of July was over. They sat quietly just holding hands.

Oliver said, "How'd you like to have three women in your family engaged?" Greta took a deep breath as she realized that he was proposing to her! She thought a minute and replied, "Do you really mean you want to marry me?" His reply was, "I've loved you since our cheap date in '38! Why wouldn't I want to marry you now?"

She was very thoughtful and then she said, "Yes, if you really want to marry at our ages."

"Let's look for a diamond ring tomorrow. We'll tell your family our good news. How would you like to take a trip to Hawaii and get married there?" By then, Greta was overwhelmed. "I've always wanted to go to Hawaii," she told him. "It sounds like a wonderful idea!"

When Greta's family heard the news, they were very surprised and, very happy that the two long-ago schoolmates would marry and live "happily ever after"—even though it took nearly 50 years to find each other.

What Happened
to the Watermelons?

Spring came early in 1937, but that only meant the dust could blow sooner than the last few years. It was the middle of the Great Depression and living in the Dust Bowl was a daily challenge.

Droughts, wind, heat and grasshoppers were daily obstacles, and the haunting question: "Will this ever end?"

A day brightener had come in early February, a moment of hope and anticipation. The colorful Gurney Seed catalog arrived in the mail. It was read cover to cover by everyone in the family. You could almost taste the homegrown tomatoes, strawberries, and corn on the cob that the catalog advertised.

The Gurney Seed Catalog Company had started serving prairie gardeners before the turn of the century. In fact, you could even order newly hatched chickens from Gurneys!

With little money for food, the seed was a great bargain. A nickel for a seed packet, free labor from the kids, and maybe by fall there would be something left to can after getting to taste the fresh vegetables during the growing season.

Albert Knox mailed in his seed order early, after hearing every family member's opinion on what should be grown in the family garden "come spring."

"Maybe it will be an above ground year," Albert told the family, expressing his theory that some years everything above ground would grow better than below ground plants. In other years, the opposite would be true. Trying to out-guess Mother Nature was almost impossible.

There was the usual seed order for radishes, cabbage, squash, potatoes, and tomatoes. Parsnips, a family favorite, would be left in the ground until after the first hard freeze and then served every Sunday as a special treat into December.

If the sweet corn grew and if there were plenty of tomatoes, there would be alot of canning so the family could have homegrown garden food throughout the late fall and winter.

The box from Gurney's arrived in early March. Its contents were sealed in glass jars so that moisture would not ruin the seed. By April, starter plants were all around the south windows of the Knox house so they would have a head start and could be planted in the garden after the threat of frost had passed.

Albert Knox set the planting deadline, "We need to be planted by Mother's Day."

"Elden, you get the manure in the wheelbarrow, spread it over the garden and mix in a few of the left-over leaves from the mulch pile. With this long drought, the ground is getting too compacted. . . harder than a banker's heart. We'll need to loosen things up to have a chance at a crop," he added. This was a veteran gardener who had learned the tricks of beating the odds of Mother Nature from his father, a homesteader who never had the luxury of buying Gurney's seed. Instead, Grandfather Knox had to rely on saving seeds from his garden every year, trading with neighbors and hoping to grow something. In good years, the gardens were lush from those seeds. In other years, they were disasters. Gurneys had produced what they called "hybrid seeds" which were more resistant to drought and insects. At least that was their claim to fame.

You could get into a pretty good Saturday night argument on Main Street whether someone's home-grown seeds were better than Gurney's seeds. In fact, at the County Fair, they had two categories for showing garden exhibits - "homegrown seeds" and "bought seeds".

The Knox family was not trying to win anything at the County Fair. They were committed to growing the best garden possible for family food. Albert Knox was willing to risk some of his hard-earned money from working at the local elevator to be sure the family got a garden in 1937.

It took two weeks after school and on weekends for Elden to hand-spade the garden. It had to be dug one spade deep and turned. Then it had to be hand-raked until it was smooth. Those were Albert's gardening rules.

"We're going to use a new technique this year called dry mulching," Albert told the family. "I heard about it from the county agent. Supposed to hold in any moisture, keep dust from blowing out of the garden and keep down the weeds."

The "keeping the weeds down" part was music to Elden's and Joycelyn's ears as they would be expected to do most of the weeding. Mrs. Knox, Vada, would help supervise the garden and would make all decisions on canning. Albert would pitch in when he could,

14

but he needed to work every possible hour at the elevator plus deliver coal to make ends meet.

By Mother's Day, the ground was all planted. Each row had been properly spaced using a "go by", a stick cut to the length the Gurney seed packets prescribed so plants would not be too crowded nor too much space left between the plants.

"Gardening is a lot like life," Albert would say. "Put the seeds in the ground, work hard, follow the rules, and then have faith the good Lord will give you a bountiful harvest."

Just like Albert said it was like a lesson in life. Hope, yet uncertainty. Would the rain come? In addition, if it did, would it bring hail to wipe out the garden? If the rain didn't come, could enough water be hauled to keep the plants alive between rains? And would an early frost kill whatever the grasshoppers missed?

"You could worry yourself to death about the crop," Albert said. But that did not fit the spirit of the hardy pioneers and their second generation that liked to say their family's best crops were "'98 and next year."

After planting the garden, Elden was instructed to use a scythe to cut old and new weeds around the ditches and down in the low-lying "weed patch" where nothing decent would grow. The cuttings were raked into piles, bundled, and placed between the garden rows to experiment with the idea of "dry mulching". This created paths of dead material between the rows.

A week after everything was planted, the first rain came. A cool spring rain that came to "eight strokes", Albert said. That was eight tenths of an inch. Not enough to grow a garden, but a good start for the season.

South of town there was no rain. Elden and Joycelyn were admonished not to brag at church that they had such a good rain in town. Everyone already knew that and bragging might be punished by no rain from the next weather front moving through. Besides, it just wasn't polite to brag.

Amazingly, the summer of '37 had more rain than during the previous six years of drought. It was still short of normal and a lot less than predicted in the official Farmer's Almanac. By the Fourth of July, the sweet corn was knee-high, the potatoes were bushy, and the family had already enjoyed homegrown carrots, onions, and radishes from the garden.

Each day Vada, Elden and Joycelyn pulled the weeds in a few rows of the garden. A little hoeing was done around some of the plants to keep the soil loose and not let the rain create a "hard pack".

Traps were set to catch rabbits and coons. The rabbits were butchered for special meals. Elden kept a lucky rabbit's foot from the first one caught, which he kept in his pocket for years. In fact, nearly all the boys carried a lucky rabbit's foot. It was no substitute for praying before going to bed, but in the "Dirty Thirties" people tried just about anything to get a better life.

There was one part in the garden that Albert took care of and asked his wife and children to leave alone.

"I'm going to try and grow some of those Gurney melons," he had told them when opening the box of seeds. "On a hot late August night right after the oats have been hauled to the elevator, a juicy melon could really hit the spot!"

In fact, Albert made a special effort in the melon growing area of the garden. He put chicken wire around it to keep out any animals. He got some sheep manure from a customer and added that to the ground for a special fertilizer. He had some white powder that a man who came by the elevator gave him to try to keep the grasshoppers and insects from eating the plants. He put a double layer of dry mulch between each melon plant. On scorching days, he rigged a canvas over the melons to keep off the hot sun and "to be prepared for a hail storm". In addition, every morning and every evening he would pump two five-gallon pails of water, carrying them all the way to the garden for the melons. Then he would dole out the water as needed, keeping the ground moist all summer long. In fact, the melons did so well by early August that neighbors would drop by to see the growth of Albert's melon crop. "Must be something in this 'dry mulching'," Alex Kruger would say. "Our garden is about as dead as a seventeen-year-old horse."

And just as the Gurney seed catalog had predicted with its lush pictures of full-grown melons, the Knox's had a beautiful crop: first the cantaloupe, then some muskmelon, and finally, the watermelon. All Albert's work had paid off with the family having fresh melons each evening in late August and throughout September. Three large melons were left in the patch, which Albert said were special and had to stay until the first freeze.

The rest of the garden also did well. The "above ground" vegetables like the tomatoes and sweet corn provided plenty to eat. Vada put up a record number of canned vegetables in glass jars. All the hard work during the summer in the garden had paid off for the Knox family. In fact, they had extra to give Pastor Knutson and his family, plus some extra vegetables for the Widow Barnes who was struggling so, that she didn't even have electric lights. Several times during the year, the county welfare agent had to bring her a few staples. It was rumored that she might have to move to the county poor farm by winter. That was a farm operated by the county for people who could not afford a house and hadn't enough money for food. It

17

was the forerunner to nursing homes, assisted living facilities, food pantries, and homeless shelters all wrapped into one.

One noon after the news, WNAX radio, ironically owned by the Gurney family, broke into special programming by Lawrence Welk and his orchestra with a weather bulletin, that a hard freeze would hit during the night, October 10th.

The whole family worked late into the night by kerosene lantern, getting the last of any vegetables from the garden. Even late-arriving green tomatoes were harvested. They were hung by their roots from the garage ceiling beam, with hope they would ripen for a last taste of vine-ripened tomatoes.

Albert said to leave the special melons, as they need to stay until the first freeze according to Gurneys.

As the family went to bed, exhausted from the "hard freeze" preparations, Albert finished getting the wood stoves ready to be lit in the morning for heat and cooking breakfast. He was the last to go to bed.

As the sun came up, Elden was the first to notice as he looked out the window towards the garden. "The melons are gone! All gone!" he said, almost ready to cry. But big boys were taught not to cry.

Vada chimed in, "What could have happened to them? Albert, see if there were any Gypsies through town last night."

"Ask the depot agent if he saw any hobos straying around town."

"I can't believe someone would steal our melons!" Joycelyn said. "We were generous all summer with what we had. Everyone knew how proud Dad has been of his crop."

Albert said nothing. He just finished breakfast with a stoic look and then headed off to work. After a few days of Vada and the children asking around, speculation about the missing melons died down.

Halloween came and the next day was a bright, sunny, calm day. Albert got the family to help "burn the garden" after church. This required putting kerosene along one end and letting the fire burn across, pushed by a little breeze, to kill all the weeds and re-fertilize the soil.

"Just like the prairie fires helped the prairie, burning the garden is nature's way," Albert would instruct. "It'll help us get it going again next year."

Then came Thanksgiving, the first snow, and the family highlight of the year, Christmas.

This year there would be a Christmas tree made out of a dead limb holding evergreen boughs placed into holes drilled with a brace and bit. The family decorations were put on the tree. Christmas Eve, for a little while, the small candles on the tree would be lit, as the family would sing "O Tannenbaum" in their German tradition.

The family ceremony came after they had been to Christmas Eve church where each child was given an apple following the service. It was a special gift from Ike Koehn, the town banker, who survived the crash of '29 unlike the other two bankers in town. He had made an annual ritual of giving thanks with a special treat each Christmas Eve for all the children in attendance.

After church, Vada served the traditional Christmas Eve dinner of squash, mashed potatoes, gravy, and a pork roast, with pumpkin pie, just a partial menu—everything but the meat coming from the garden.

Christmas day the kids were up early to see what Santa Claus had brought. This year there was no pre-Christmas announcement that because of the drought and Depression Santa had sent a message that he

19

wouldn't be leaving anything but some big cookies. So there was anticipation of gifts this year.

As dawn came, Elden and Joycelyn bounced out of bed. Santa had come! "A rifle! Now I can shoot jackrabbits and pheasants!" Elden said. Joycelyn fought back tears as she held up a new dress that looked like it had walked right out of the Sears and Roebuck catalog and into the Knox home. And each got a new book.

They couldn't wait to go to church to tell their friends what Santa had brought.

The Christmas morning church service was nearly all Christmas carols with a short message from Pastor Knutson about "Joy in the World", even in tough times. It was a version of "Joy To The World" he adapted for the Christmas day message. Then after communion for adults and prayers for all, the Knox family headed for home.

Usually, relatives and friends would drop by unannounced, staying for a short time or a long time, depending on their schedules on Christmas Day. The kids would play checkers, marbles, or multiple players of Chinese checkers using a board with different colored marbles for each player.

But this year it was quiet most of the afternoon. Albert took Elden out to shoot at tin cans, teaching him how to use his new (used) rifle.

Vada decided to bake a cake and Joycelyn helped her in the kitchen while Vada told stories of what Christmas was like in their homestead house eight miles north of town when she grew up.

About 4:00 P.M. the Pepmuller's came over. Then some of the Knox family relatives showed up. And so did the Kruger's and the Marquardt's. By 5:30, the house was filled with friends and neighbors exchanging Christmas greetings, stories, and telling "Hoover jokes" about the Depression.

"Why he's so poor, he can't afford mice for his cat!" one neighbor cracked while talking about a farmer who lived north of town.

Albert disappeared. He was gone about ten minutes when he entered the back door grinning ear to ear. He was carrying three of the best watermelons ever grown in the territory.

"Surprise! It's time to share the Christmas melons." Albert said like a kid who discovered candy.

The women helped get out plates and sliced a melon into wedges so it could be easily eaten.

The bright red fruit was delicious. Everyone got plenty of the delicacy.

Albert finally confessed.

"When I bought my Gurney's seed this year, they had a special new hybrid melon called the "Christmas melon." It was supposed to be picked just before the first frost and then allowed to ripen in an oatbin where it would not freeze. It was bred to ripen by Christmas — which is why they call it the "Christmas melon."

"Well, I'll be," said Vada. "What will they come up with next?"

"Albert, you had us thinking those melons were stolen. I should kick you out in the snow bank for an hour for what you put us through."

Albert was unfazed. He was too happy about being able to share a special Christmas treat with his friends and neighbors.

"No, Vada. I didn't say anything the day the melons were gone. And you didn't ask if I took them. So I just decided we'd have a big Christmas surprise."

"Well, you and Gurneys really pulled one over on all of us," she said, as everyone burst out singing "For He's a Jolly Good Fellow."

A Memorable Memorial Day

Almost in a tie with Good Friday, Decoration Day, which became Memorial Day held on May 30th, was the most somber day of the year.

Since 1868, when General John Logan of the Grand Army of the Republic (GAR) declared each May 30th as a day to decorate the graves of deceased soldiers, Americans have been honoring the memories of those who made the ultimate sacrifice in war. They commemorated this day with parades, ceremonies, speeches and decorating graves.

At first southern states resisted celebrating the day believing it to be held for Union soldiers. But after World War I, all states recognized the day. Then Congress changed the official date in 1968 to the last Monday in May creating a three-day weekend. This has led to a few states celebrating different dates; some fiercely maintaining the traditional May 30th date and others the federally established day.

Each town had a little different tradition for Memorial Day. Some had a parade which moved toward its conclusion at the local cemetery. Others had programs in an outdoor amphitheater, at the courthouse, or on the courthouse veranda and then progressed to a designated cemetery. Still others held the entire ceremony at a cemetery.

A typical Memorial Day in Ridgeway was planned during months of committee discussion and debate. This year's parade would form at the local high school. It would go through three blocks of Main Street, stop at the local bridge and then move a half-mile out of town to the local cemetery for final ceremonies. The location would alternate each year between the Protestant and Catholic areas of the cemetery as a symbol of inter-denominational cooperation.

The parade would be led by Veterans of Foreign Wars (VFW) color guard. After World War I, the VFW claimed this right by the fact they all served overseas compared to the American Legion who allowed any uniformed veteran to join.

The VFW was followed by the GAR delegation, which were veterans, siblings or descendants of Union Civil War soldiers.

Next came any Spanish American War veterans or spouses who were still alive. Ridgeway had one such vet, Hugh Stoddard. Hugh would ride in the parade each year in his Model T shined in glistening black. He would rub linseed oil on the tires to make them shine for at least a day. Behind Hugh came the World War I veterans who marched in three columns led by a retired captain, a survivor of a mustard gas attack by the Kaiser's Army in France. Marching alongside and shouting orders, Captain Porter's purple heart and rank gave him the unwritten authority to command the veterans of the "war to end all wars" in the Memorial Day Parade. The school band was scheduled next. The snare drums were adjusted so the drumbeat could be heard only in muffled sounds. The bass drum would be hit once then a muffled snare drum three times to create a "hut, two, three, four" marching cadence slower than the usual parade cadence. This was fol-lowed by a host of vehicles, a hay wagon carrying

23

American Legion Auxiliary chorus and a special car for the dignitaries who would be speaking this year. Reverend Knust from the Methodist Church would be giving the invocation and the benediction at the ceremony. Congressman Burlington, rumored to be a future candidate for the U.S. Senate, would give the main address. Retired Colonel Benjamin Forseth would present a short message entitled "We Were Privileged to Fight and Die for You."

Another car would carry the local English teacher. Miss Irene McMaster would be doing her annual reading of the poem "In Flanders Field" written to commemorate those who made the ultimate sacrifice in the Great War. This would be followed by her explanation of Poppy Days.

Others of lesser rank would join to complete the parade. A riderless horse led by a uniformed Army veteran in recognition of the fallen Cavalry soldiers would conclude the parade.

It was hoped that the horse would not bolt at the cemetery when the 21-gun salute was fired, like it did two years ago destroying many decorations on the graves.

The parade would make its way through Main Street past the new electric light poles, draped with black crepe paper flowing from each as a makeshift ribbon. All the flags from the school to the post office and Masonic Temple plus the courthouse would be at half-mast.

The procession would halt at the bridge while flowers and wreaths would be thrown into the river followed by a 21-gun salute, seven vets firing three times each almost in unison. That would commemorate those who died at sea including those who silently said under their breath "remember The Lusitania."

The Memorial Day parade would then make its way to the cemetery. A platform made from a hay wagon would become a temporary stage trimmed in red, white and blue bunting. Large wooden chairs with leather seats borrowed from the Elk's Lodge would be on the hay wagon for the main speakers. The Presbyterian Church podium would be placed center stage. There would be room for the American Legion Auxiliary Chorus to sing. And upon arrival, one of the bands better trumpet players would head for the grove of trees near the cemetery to play the "echo" during Taps. The only real significant variables from year to year in the Ridgeway Memorial Day Program were the invocation and the benediction, depending on which clergy would be asked to deliver these messages. The main speaker would be asked to prepare at least one hour on the meaning of war, patriotism and being an American. Anything short of an hour would be deemed inadequate. One time, the main speaker went for two hours and thirteen minutes, a record. The townspeople would still recall this epic speech of Judge Warren, who had set a high standard for the Memorial Day addresses.

The American Auxiliary Chorus would first sing *The Battle Hymn of the Republic*. The school band would play its featured number, Dovorak's *Going Home*. The final chorus piece would be *America The Beautiful*. Of course, the band would also play the *Star Spangled Banner* and *Stars and Stripes Forever* furnish trumpet players for Taps, and leave playing the *Funeral March*. Miss Irene McMaster would be called upon to read, just before the introduction of the main speaker by the mayor, *In Flanders Field*, a poem written by a Canadian Army doctor. She would carefully enunciate:

"In Flanders field, the poppies blow

Between the crosses, row by row
That mark our place, and in the sky,
The larks still bravely singing, fly,
Scarce heard amid the guns below.
We are the Dead. Short days ago
We lived, felt dawn, saw sunset glow,
Loved, and were loved, and now we lie
In Flanders field.
Take up our quarrel with the foe!
To you from failing hands we throw
The torch; be yours to hold it high!
If ye break faith with us to die
We shall not sleep, though poppies grow
In Flanders Field."

Miss McMaster would follow this with an explanation of why red poppies were sold by local veterans and worn on Memorial Day. She would annually relate *In Flander's Field* inspired an American poet, Moira Michael, to write a sequel poem:

"We cherish, too, the Poppy red
That grows on fields where valour led.
It seems to signal to the skies
That blood of heroes never dies,"

And Miss McMaster would remind the gathered crowd that their purchases of artificial poppies would help disabled veterans in need of additional financial support. Frankly, it was unpatriotic not to wear one.

The setting would be complete with the cemetery mowed to perfection, all trees trimmed of their dead branches, and the graves decorated with wreaths, flowers and ribbons, commemorating the lives served for others.

Year after year, with minor adjustments, the same Memorial Day parade and ceremony would be repeated. Perhaps if this repetition of the program would further emblazon the importance of the occasion in the minds of younger generations, we might appreciate the sacrifices of those who had fought for freedom. The annual plans were all in place for another day of remembrance.

AND THEN CAME MEMORIAL DAY, 1941

The rain started on the evening of the 29th. It poured! Just what the farmer said was needed to "break the drought" for good. It rained steadily until the morning. At 11:00 A.M., the mayor made the decision after conferring with all involved, that the Memorial Day ceremonies of 1941 would be moved inside to the school gym. It was simply too wet and muddy to attempt an outdoor ceremony. The arguments of the majority to move inside had their opponents. A handful said if the Great War vets had to fight in the rain, the least those who benefited from their sacrifice could do was to conduct the Memorial Day ceremony in the rain. But they lost to those choosing a dry, indoor ceremony.

Plans were quickly altered. The big chairs from The Elks would still be used. So would the Presbyterian podium. Bunting would be put along the stage.

The dignitaries would march in single file from one door to the gym. The school band would come in from the other door. The outside doors to the gym would be opened briefly to hear the 21-gun salute, plus Taps with the echo. Perhaps the speech by Congressman Burlington would make this day even more special, as it was a rare appearance in Ridgeway by such a high ranking elected official. The lilacs had bloomed early, so two large baskets were placed on each side of the stage. The stage looked good for a makeshift event with hardly any committee meetings on the decisions.

Before the ceremonies, the band director had a special lecture to the band about not hitting any "sour notes." These would be heard more easily indoors than outdoors. There was an extra stern message about remaining solemn to match the gravity of the day set aside to remember the dead. "Do not even think of smiling," he warned.

By program time, the gym was filled from the bleachers with younger families and children to the chairs on the main floor with a colorful variety of veterans. Boy and Girl Scouts, some veterans with their service caps, and a few veterans stuffed into their uniforms, all wearing red poppies, added color to the event. After the dignitaries and the American Legion Auxiliary Chorus had arrived at their appointed places, it was time for the local band to enter the gym. They would be led by the official VFW color guard as a prelude to posting the colors and playing of *The National Anthem.*

As already planned, the band's majorette, petite Marilyn Moore, in a short skirt and white boots, blew her whistle and the procession began with a slow, solemn pace as the band marched to the muffled drumbeats. Preceeding the band, an elderly VFW flag bearer approached the front of the gym. The band marked time to the roll of the drums. The Commander called, "Halt." Then "Advance Colors." This command meant the flag bearers would place the flags on each side of the stage, in waiting holders, and then take their seats in reserved chairs in the front row. Each flag bearer advanced toward the stage. The American Flag bearer felt a tug. He quickly realized that the eagle emblem on the top of the flag standard met the mesh of the basketball hoop, which hung from the north end of the stage. With frustration and embarrassment, the flag bearer gave the flag a sharp twist to the left and a quick jerk to the right, in an effort to disengage the flag. But disaster had already struck! It was securely entwined! His color-bearing partner placed his flagstick in the proper receptacle, and then came over to assist with the problem. However, their efforts were to no avail. A quick thinking member of the audience ran to the boiler room searching for a ladder, stool, or anything to help untangle the flag. But the custodian had considered it a holiday, locked everything tightly and had gone fishing up north. The would-be hero returned to the gym with hand and facial gestures signifying failure. Silence was maintained for a time, with just a crying baby bringing a sound to the auditorium. The band watched with its practiced discipline. At first they were wide eyed and restrained. The clarinet player began to giggle. That did it! The trombone section had their faces in their mouthpieces, the tubas hid behind their huge horns. The others tried to stare at the floor to keep from laughing. The director signaled the band to play *America The Beautiful*. It was ragged and rough, but it alleviated the situation slightly while the veterans continued to try untangling the flag from the basketball net.

As the entwined flag became more hopelessly embedded, all efforts were abandoned. The distraught VFW colorguard sank into their chairs and left the flag and pole hanging limply from the hoop. The attached flag swung slightly in the gentle airflow. The program progressed with an invocation and eventually to Congressman Burlington who made a remark intended to bring humor to the situation. It brought an uproarious laughter of relief from the audience. There was little concentration on the rest of his remarks. The band members had to struggle to sit still in their chairs, not look up, not laugh, and especially not look at each other. It was a major challenge for this batch of youngsters, as well as the audience. After the ceremonies concluded, the band struggled to go through the *Stars and Stripes Forever.* Then they led the recession out of the gym, attempting to play the *Funeral March.*

Total pandemonium broke out as a little five-year-old pointed and yelled, "Hey, you forgot to take down the flag!"

By Memorial Day, 1942, the country was back at war. Nothing seemed to be funny. However, after the war, each Memorial Day former band members and others relived the ceremony of 1941 — when the American flag incident dominated Memorial Day because the flag was "still there."

THE GOOD LORD
HAS BLESSED
US RICHLY

The Minister's Wife
Didn't need Santa!

Emma Miller heard the church bells ringing and realized that the Christmas Eve service would begin within minutes. She hurried to find her hat and coat but stopped to peek into the oven of her black, cast iron kitchen range. The coffeecakes were not quite done. She fumed to herself, "If I had a decent stove those cakes would have been brown twenty minutes ago! The grates are so bad, the fuel will not burn right and all I have is many ashes to haul outside. If I believed in Santa Claus, I know the first thing on my list!"

She took the sweet breads out of the oven and turned them out on the breadboard. "I guess they'll do" she said to herself. "One never knows who'll come home from church with us or how many people will stop by, as it is Christmas Eve."

Just before going out the door, Emma grabbed her wet mop and wiped up tracks made by melted snow near the kitchen door. She hid the mop and pail behind the pantry door and bundled up into her coat.

Before she reached the door, there was a brisk knocking on the other side. "WHO NOW?" she wondered in frustration. "The service is ready to start and I cannot be delayed. Reverend will notice I am not in my pew and our children will worry. I wouldn't have been

31

so far behind today if Mettie Kalebearer hadn't spent two hours visiting this afternoon," she stewed.

Emma opened the door and her eyes fell on a young couple dressed in Sunday clothes. They appeared nervous and excited.

The young man tipped his gray Fedora hat and inquired, "Is the Reverend at home?"

"I'm sorry," Emma replied, "he's at church as the Christmas Eve program is ready to begin. In fact, the bells have already rung."

"But we came to be married!" said the petite blonde girl who was wearing a white Angora tam which blew feather-like in the breeze. "When will the service be finished?" asked the groom.

Emma sized up the situation quickly. It was not uncommon during the depression to skip big church weddings and be married at a parsonage to save the expenses of a formal wedding. Many weddings had been performed in her parlor.

"Why don't the two of you come with me to the service? As soon as it is over, the Reverend will come right back here and marry you. Do you have a license?" They nodded in unison.

The pair looked at each other with some apprehension, which was easily interpreted by Emma. They would rather skip the service. Emma became insistent. "If you come right now, I'm sure you can find room in the balcony as the choir and children will be marching from the basement tonight. They will then sit in the reserved seats in the sanctuary. You can sit upstairs near the organ and see everything. No one will pay attention to you. Hurry! Follow me!"

The couple had little choice but trail the pastor's wife through the light snow to the church on the corner of the block. The young man hung tightly to his girl as her high heels were clicking along in Emma's path. As the trio passed the big evergreen trees, which practically blocked the sidewalk, they smelled the fragrant balm emitting from the trees. Clumps of snow clung to their branches and a full moon lit their path.

They followed Emma up the front steps of the church into the brilliantly lit narthex. Emma motioned to a short flight of stairs just inside the church entry. The couple tiptoed upstairs and disappeared into the church balcony. The organist and young man with a trumpet paid no attention to them.

Emma, breathless, tried to walk slowly and sedately down the far aisle of the church almost hugging the candle-lit windows. She slid into her seat in the front row. Her appearance went unnoticed as simultaneously the organ began a swell of joyful notes and a trumpet sounded. A parade of children, followed by the adult choir, burst out singing the familiar Christmas hymns, *Joy to the World!* and *O, Little Town of Bethlehem.*

The Christmas tree, almost reaching to the ceiling, was bright with little colored lights and the branches were heavy with colorful balls, popcorn and cranberry strings. "Every year the church looks more beautiful," Emma thought. "We are lucky that Ernest has such a big church and faithful congregation, as Cedarburg is just a small town in a farm community."

The singing procession came to the front and filed into the reserved sections. She noticed her own children, eyes glistening, and their hearts intent on their singing. Her sons, Carl and Albert, looked neat in their Sunday suits although both of their suits were snug. She had worked hard to remake dresses for Rose Marie and Elizabeth Ann and the added ruffles and ribbons made the girls' dresses as pretty as their friends' store bought ones. "Maybe better," she consoled herself.

She was jolted out of her thoughts as she heard her husband's resonant voice read the Christmas story according to the Gospel of St. Luke. The beautiful message embodied the entire message of Christmas. Emma watched her handsome husband and thought, "He is as conscientious as his name, "Ernest" implies. No wonder the parishioners have been so good to us this past year. 1940 has been a better year for crops. Prices are low but farmers have been generous in giving our family supplies to see us in food." Also, she gave thanks that Ernest had been voted a small salary raise. She was deep in thought and prayer when she realized the congregation was singing, *Hark! The Herald Angels Sing*, one of her favorite hymns.

As the congregation continued to sing, Emma stole a quick glance backward into the choir loft and spotted the heads of the two strangers who were eager to have Reverend Miller marry them. "May the Lord bless them and touch their hearts with His love," she prayed.

Emma became sleepy as she smelled the light smoke from the candles in the church windows, the boughs of the Christmas tree and felt the warmth of the furnace heat seeping from the big radiators along the sides of the church. She also smelled whiffs of Evening in Paris perfume worn by some of the older girls who dabbed it behind their ears. This special perfume was reserved for holidays and special occasions, she knew. Her girls were too young for such teenage experimentation.

Despite the solemnity of the occasion, the manger scene with Baby Jesus in a crib of hay, the shepherds coming down the aisle in their crude costumes, wise men in bright bathrobes carrying versions of gold, myrrh and frankincense, recitations and songs, the pastor's wife's mind was busy sorting out the events of the day. She tried to wake up by organizing her thoughts about the wedding to be held at the parsonage after the service.

Emma remembered vividly the conversation that afternoon between herself and neighbor, Mettie, who sat at her kitchen table, drinking coffee and mixing complaints, gossip and bragging. Mettie had come to complain that Elizabeth Ann had told her little Emily that there was not a Santa Claus. "Christmas was Jesus' birthday," Elizabeth Ann had told her daughter. It had upset Emily and spoiled her Christmas.

"In OUR church, we have Christmas service on Christmas DAY and afterwards Santa comes and brings treats for all us" Mettie declared.

Emma had continued baking and washing dishes while Mettie drank more coffee and bragged about the new stove HER man had given her for Christmas. In addition, she shared that Marvel and Emily were the most popular girls in school, and how much business her husband had in his hardware store.

Emma remembered the Bible verse "Love one another" but sometimes her neighbor's bragging made it hard to live up to that lesson, especially on Christmas Eve day when she had much to do. She offered a prayer for patience with Mettie.

She was jolted to reality when the service ended with the beautiful hymn, *The First Noel*. Then the Sunday School children walked to the front of the altar to sing *Silent Night, Holy Night* with small candles the only light.

As the children were ushered out of the cloakroom, ushers handed each child a brown paper sack. They knew what it contained remembering the other years, but they took a peek to make sure. Inside there were peanuts in the shell, an apple, an orange and kaleidoscope colored hard candy pieces. The ushers told them to wait until they got home to eat it. What a temptation that was for the young children.

When Emma was finally ushered out, the minister was still shaking hands and receiving holiday greetings from his parishioners. The would-be newlyweds were waiting patiently in the doorway to talk to the minister about getting married.

"Would people ever leave?" she asked herself. She was anxious to get home to put cobs in the stove to make coffee for the couple after their marriage. People kept shaking her hand and visiting until she had a feeling she was being unnecessarily detained. Her husband was still surrounded by people but she excused herself and pushed through to whisper in her husband's ear about the couple waiting to be married. She introduced the pair, he told them to go home with Emma, and he would be there as soon as possible.

As Emma, her children and the marriage couple, Mary Alice and Andrew, approached the parsonage, they were amazed. Every light in the house was on! Emma gasped! She did NOT leave lights on! They also noticed foot prints and tire tracks in the snow leading up to the kitchen door. The door was ajar and people were inside. She nearly fainted as Ernest came running up behind her.

Simultaneously the family pushed through the kitchen door. Friends and neighbors were jammed into the kitchen and were shouting, "Merry Christmas!"

The old, black iron cook stove was gone! Evaporated! Disappeared! In its place was a beautiful, white copper clad range, aglow with a brisk fire and a teakettle singing a merry song. "Where?" "How?"

"A gift from the congregation!" was the answer. Ernest and Emma were speechless. The children were using the handles to lift the lids and see the blazing fire.

Everyone was talking. Mettie was mopping up the last of the soot made from taking out the old stove. "How did the men handle those hot pipes?" asked Pastor Miller, as he knew his wife had been baking before the service. The answer from the men, "Very carefully!"

The kitchen table was laden with holiday food: cakes, pies, cookies, sandwiches, krumkaka, lefsa, fruitcake...a groaning board of holiday goodies. People were outside trying to get in. Finally, the decision was made to take things to the church kitchen and enjoy coffee and fellowship there.

Pastor Miller introduced the bewildered couple. Since they wanted to have a private wedding as soon as possible, the congregation left for the church.

Rose Marie ran into the parlor to find Lohengrin's *Bridal March* in the organ bench. She had played for weddings before and was excited about being home to play for this wedding.

Several ladies were fastening pine boughs over the archway between the living room and parlor. Mettie was stirring a coffee and egg mixture into the family coffeepot filled with boiling water. It bubbled and the aroma permeated the house.

Pastor Miller was visiting with the groom and examining the marriage license. All seemed in order. The bride asked for time to comb her hair and drink some water. The groom also wanted to brush his hair and catch his breath. Emma clipped a blossom from her Christmas cactus and pinned it on Mary Alice's dress. "A bride needs flowers," she said.

The bride and groom stood in the archway as candles flickered on the table and Rose Marie played the organ briefly. The service began as the pastor read the marriage service. The vows were exchanged and the groom slipped a ring on the bride's finger. The pastor pronounced them married and added; "You may kiss the bride," as he nodded to the groom. Albert tittered and Rose Marie watched with amazement as the couple kissed.

Emma invited the pair to stay and eat with them but they were anxious to leave. The couple thanked the pastor and said they would never, ever forget Christmas 1940 and the blessings they felt from the Christmas Eve service.

As the couple was putting on their coats to leave, the groom pressed an envelope into the minister's hand and said, "Thank you!" Emma kissed the bride.

Mettie was wrapping sandwiches, cookies and candy and packed them into a brown grocery sack. She put the sack into the couple's car as the newlyweds sped off into the moonlit night.

Ernest, Emma, Carl, Albert, Rose Marie and Elizabeth Ann and Mettie went back to the church to enjoy lunch and fellowship with parishioners. Pastor Miller gave a "thank you" to the congregation for the wonderful gift of the new kitchen stove. People left soon as they wanted to be home for their own family Christmas Eve.

When the parsonage was finally quiet and the children in bed, the clock struck midnight. Ernest and Emma pulled kitchen chairs in front of the new stove to enjoy the warmth. They opened the oven door, took off their shoes and put their tired feet on the warm oven door.

Ernest reached into his pocket for a handkerchief to wipe a tear from his eyes. The envelope, given to him by the groom, fell onto the floor. He retrieved it, tore it open and found a $20 bill inside, a bonanza during the depression! Emma looked at the stove, the money and her husband and said, "Maybe just for a minute, you would think there was a Santa Claus."

"Think what a tale Mettie will have to tell tomorrow. No wonder the townspeople have nick-named her Mrs. Tale-bearer," Ernest said. "But," Emma replied, "Mettie really helped out tonight with making coffee and cleaning the kitchen after the new stove was brought in. We needed her help. She knows where everything is in this kitchen."

"The Good Lord has blessed us richly," said Ernest. He planted a long, tender kiss on his wife's glowing cheeks. "It's a Christmas Eve we'll never forget."

SKIP DAY
SANDWHICHES
ONLY 25¢ !!

BUY OUR BUNS.
WE NEED
YOUR DOUGH!

The 1940 High School Senior Class Unforgettable Skip Day

The traditional Wentworth Corn Days celebration held every October brought many visitors to this small town during the 1940's and '50's. The 4-H club members exhibited their best projects for awards. Women's clubs and individuals displayed quilts and embroidery items. The fire hall on Main Street was filled with crafts and crop items such as corn, oats, rye, baked and canned goods and garden flowers. Prizes were awarded for the best of each category.

Free watermelon slices were a huge attraction. Barrels of ice water contained large, ripe watermelons. Children and adults stood in line for their big slice of this delicious fruit. Usually the melons only lasted until early evening but there was plenty of entertainment on the carnival midway.

A large carnival filled Main Street with a Ferris wheel, merry-go-round and game stands of every kind. The fortuneteller's tent enticed adults who believed or disbelieved in the gypsy's mystic. The combined attractions swelled the population to several times its normal population.

By early evening farmers had milked their cows, picked the eggs and had come to Wentworth to sell their eggs and cream. The money was used to buy groceries and enjoy the carnival. Teenagers were doing

40

what was known as "making hay while the sun shines." They were riding the Ferris wheel and playing carnival ball games set up in small tents. Many were convinced that they could beat the "carnies" game. However, usually they spent their money and did not receive any of the enticing prizes. The children spent their money on carnival rides and for penny candy sold in the grocery stores. Five-cent ice cream cones were also a favorite treat.

Adults could play a game called BINGO. The cost was a quarter a game but prizes were quilts, household decorations, carnival glass and jewelry. Some people spent most of the evening entranced by this game of chance.

People also came to eat something different from their usual home cooking. The Wentworth senior class traditionally had a booth to sell hot dogs and hamburgers for Corn Days. They needed the money for their secret skip day in the spring. With the meat sold to them at wholesale prices from Jake's Grocery and the Old Home Bread Company donating day-old buns, they could sell their sandwiches for $.25 each.

The sign on their booth read: HELP THE SENIORS; BUY OUR BUNS!

WE NEED YOUR DOUGH!

High school seniors kept busy frying hamburgers and cooking hotdogs using an old kerosene stove. It sat on a wobbly table in a small tent. The girls did not want to fry meat for fear of getting their good clothes dirty. Eddie, Eugene, and several other boys said they would fry if the girls would take orders, put the money in a tin can, and watch so the customers did not use more than one paper napkin.

An early customer, "Mrs. Crab" the kids had silently named her, complained that her hamburger was burned. When they gave her another one, she said it was not done. The boys told her that she was too fussy. Their frying pan was old and the stove heat was hard to control but they did their best to please customers.

"Mrs. Crab" walked home and brought the group a big heavy iron pan and fresh lard for them to use. "Here's my contribution to your "skip day" fund," she said. Their business picked up rapidly. The quarter burgers began to sell like "hot cakes." The money tin began to fill.

During the event, all the Wentworth teachers stopped by for a sandwich or to visit. Superintendent Smith (students called him "Soup") also came by and offered to help. "He's a good guy," Eddie observed.

As night approached, Supt. Smith took the money tin home. The senior class would meet on Monday to pay for the meat and calculate how much money would be available for the spring Skip Day. They estimated that they had sold about 200 sandwiches which would be $50; plenty for Skip Day in May.

Two of the senior girls, Rosie and Gerry, took the fry pan back to Mrs. Thomas and thanked her for the help. The fry pan was in bad shape and would take a lot of homemade soap, elbow grease and water to clean it. She told them that she liked helping young people. The girls reported Mrs. Thomas should no longer be thought of as "Mrs. Crab."

As the night grew later some people started home. But the high school boys and their girlfriends were not ready to call it a day. Madison was only eight miles away on a paved road. The high school boys who lived in town were able to use the family cars for dates and movies. Their friends piled into the cars and headed for Madison to catch the late movies. There were two theaters showing second movies at 10:00 P.M. for only a dime. They could also buy fresh popcorn for a nickel and pop for a dime.

The two theaters were near each other. The Lyric Theater movies appealed to the boys as the shows were often of cowboys and what they called "root'n-toot'n shoot'n" stories. The more romantic movies were shown at the Crystal Theatre where the girls enjoyed seeing their favorite actresses and actors.

The Wentworth cars parked on Main Street between the two theaters near the popcorn wagon and city drinking fountain. The boys and a few girls bought tickets at the Lyric Theater but most of the girls hurried to get tickets at the Crystal Theater as the time for late movies approached.

At the Lyric Theater was a 1938 film *Boys Town* with Father Flanagan played by Spencer Tracy. It was a true story of a priest who opened a national home and school for homeless boys, Boys Town, located near Omaha, Nebraska. The boys were happy to know there was a place for these unfortunate boys. They also felt fortunate to be living with their parents and siblings. Life was good, they decided after seeing this film.

It was nearly midnight when the girls came out of the Crystal Theater. They were laughing and bubbling with delight as they talked about the movie, *Babes in Arms* with Judy Garland in the lead singing romantic songs. The girls sang and hummed the new songs enroute home.

Sunday morning came early for the tired teenagers who would be going to church and Sunday School when their chores were done. However, the annual Corn Days celebration had been a great time; one they would always remember.

Monday morning the school bell rang and the students stood at attention to recited the Pledge of Allegiance to the American Flag. Then they went to classes. During the noon hour, the seniors went to Supt. Smith's office to count the Corn Days concession money. With an estimate of the bill for the meat, the balance was $50, just as they had speculated. That would be plenty of money for their Skip Day plus buying corsages for the girl graduates in May, 1940.

Supt. Smith told Arvin and Gerry, class president and vice-president, to pay the bills and deposit the money in the Dakota State Bank. He said they would receive 3% yearly interest on the money.

Basketball games, poetry contests, Halloween, school plays, Christmas and Easter vacations came and went rapidly for the Wentworth senior class. The junior class was already making plans to host the senior class banquet and dance. The 1940 senior class found themselves in a quandary thinking about their future as graduation was fast approaching.

The senior class met in Supt. Smith's office several times to pick an appropriate day for "Skip Day." They finally decided that the first Friday in May would be perfect unless it rained or the weather was unusually cold. May days were usually very pleasant but their trip could be changed if the weather were undesirable.

Finally, May came.

On Thursday several of the senior girls stayed after school until all other students had left. They used large pieces of chalk to write notices on the classroom blackboards for lower class students to read the next morning: "TODAY IS SKIP DAY!" "WE WILL CELE-BRATE!" "SEE YOU MONDAY!" "WE ARE LUCKY DUCKS!"

Supt. Smith would drive his car with Eddie and Arvin driving their family cars. They were thankful for three good cars. Most families had only one car which dad drove. A few farmers had a grain or cattle truck to use at home when their sons wanted the car. Very few women drove cars in the 1940's. Cars were for men to drive.

The planned route to Sioux Falls was east to Lone Tree and then south on Highway #77. That was a paved road, which went through Dell Rapids, then toward Sioux Falls past the State Prison and overlooked the big John Morrell Meat Processing plant. Both places would be interesting to tour, they had decided.

A hitchhiker held up his thumb begging for a ride but since their cars were full, the man would have to bum a ride with another southbound car. Besides, the day was beautiful with no wind so there was no reason to pick up the stranger. In the middle of winter, they might have squeezed him in because, "Who knows, next time it could be one of us needing a ride," Arvin said.

Superintendent Smith's car, the leader of the three-car caravan, slowed. He honked his horn once, rolled down his car window, and pointed his finger at the driveway on the right side. As they stopped in front of the building, they realized that this was the State Penitentiary. Smith got out of his car and told the rest to wait while he inquired if the group could visit the prison. Each person in the car almost held their breath in anticipation of this experience.

The Superintendent came out and knocked on the car windows to say that juveniles were not welcome unless they were there to see a family member. Since no one had family members doing time, that was that.

The next possibility was a visit to the John Morrell Meatpacking Plant, which was located across the road and down a steep hill from the prison. By the time the cars were heading in that direction, the odor from the packing plant almost made the group gag. The trio of cars finally drove around long enough to find an office door. Trucks of all sizes were lined up in one area of the many buildings. There were sounds of animals making weird noises and the girls were ready to jump out of the cars and run up the hill. They had not planned to tour a place that smelled so bad.

Supt. Smith told the group to wait while he talked to the manager. He was gone quite awhile but came to explain the situation. The office people told him that the boys may want to walk through the building to observe their process of killing cattle, cleaning and cutting the flesh and watch the lines of workers doing their part in the operation.

However, they suggested that the girls come into the office and wait. It would be cool in their waiting room and they could listen to the big radio while waiting for the boys. This was agreeable, as the smell was not evident in the office headquarters.

The radio was very large and there was a good program on from WNAX Radio, Yankton, S.D. A group called "The Six Fat Dutchmen" was playing polka music followed by a band of fiddlers. Soon a clerk brought them a Coke to drink. The girls were relaxed and happy that they had declined the tour.

The male group did not spend much time looking at the hog and beef operation of killing, cleaning and processing meat. They looked a little pale and were ready to leave as soon as possible. They made no comments but knew they would have a lot to tell when they got home.

The next stop was downtown Sioux Falls to the well-known Phillips Avenue with stores on both sides of the street and people walking the sidewalks. Since it was time to eat a noon meal, they found parking places and met on the corner at the Schriver building. Most of them had been in Sioux Falls in the past but several had never seen the shopping area.

A block south from Schrivers was a corner building advertising: "NICKEL PLATE...ALL YOU CAN EAT!" That sounded good to the hungry boys who decided it would be better to eat hamburger than hotdogs, based on their Morrell tour. They decided to eat noon lunch there but the girls discussed eating at Schriver's Tea Room on fourth floor of the big department store or at Fantle's well known restaurant down a block on Main Avenue where some said their mothers like to eat when shopping in Sioux Falls.

The beautiful Carpenter Hotel was across the street and in the middle of the block. Smith gave each of them $3.00 to pay for the noon lunch and asked them to meet at the hotel lobby at 2:00 P.M. This would give them time to eat and look over the businesses including checking the movie theaters' advertising.

The boys went to the Nickel Plate and the girls upstairs to the Schriver's Tea Room. To their surprise, a woman dressed like a gypsy told the girls that she could read their fortune if they drank tea. She could predict their future by the shape of the tea leaves in the bottom of their cup. The cost was 50 cents. After discussion, they decided their parents would not like the idea and that they would rather spend the money for dessert. There were so many choices of cake, pie, bars and Jell-O desserts in all colors. The array of pies produced mass indecision: apple, pumpkin, banana, cherry, mincemeat, pecan and many others that could be ordered with whipped cream topping. The cost of a piece of pie was 25 cents, so they were happy they did not fall for the tea leaf fortuneteller, leaving enough money for pie.

The girls looked at all the dresses in the downtown store windows and the boys checked out the other stores. By 2:00 P.M. the group met in the lobby of the Carpenter Hotel as planned. It was a very luxurious place. They felt like spending time there to relax or maybe take a quick nap on the upholstered chairs and sofas.

Superintendent Smith had an announcement when they were thinking that their fun was about over. He told them they would be leaving for Dell Rapids! This rekindled their excitement as they responded almost in unison: "WHY DELL RAPIDS?" Superintendent Smith then asked them, "How many of you would like to roller-skate with a background of popular music?" That sounded good, as the Dells Park was a beautiful place along the Big Sioux River.

"I have made arrangements with the park director to open the pavilion at 4:00 P.M. so you can roller-skate, and some of the Dells students will join you." All of a sudden their tiredness disappeared and they were anxious to head for "Dells."

"And," he continued, "that is not all! We will be staying for the evening to attend a wonderful movie in the Dells Theater tonight. You will be surprised when you find out the name of the show!"

The trip from Sioux Falls to Dell Rapids was only 30 miles. Skip Day was getting more exciting than they had imagined. They liked roller-skating and they could almost smell the popcorn. "And a movie tonight!!" was their excited response.

The skating was great. They made new friends with Dells students who came to skate. The popcorn and Coke kept their spirits high! But what about the movie? Why did the Superintendent talk as if it was a really big event?

At 5:30 P.M. the skaters were getting hungry and wondered where they would be eating. Hamburgers were getting a little tiresome. The group was taken to an interesting café near the river called the Dutch Inn. The menu listed many interesting items including pork, beef with scalloped potatoes and ham. The table had a white cloth, napkins and pretty flowers for decoration. "This is really living!" said one of the boys who had never eaten in such a nice restaurant.

With plenty to eat and money left for the movie, they drove to the east end of Dell Rapids main street. The theater was aglow with lights and people were lined up outside waiting for the doors to open. Bright signs and pictures were on the front and sides of the building: *GONE WITH THE WIND!* Vivian Leigh and Clark Gable!

The Skip Day seniors were able to find good seats near the front since they were in line early enough. Superintendent Smith paid for the tickets and did not tell them that this show cost 50 cents each. To everyone's surprise, the movie was in Technicolor! This was new, as they had only seen black and white movies. Unbelievable!

The movie was the best any of them could imagine with Clark Gable playing the role of Rhett Butler and Vivian Leigh as Scarlett O'Hara. The movie would eventually win more Oscar Awards that any movie ever written. It was the only story written by Margaret Mitchell, who was killed in a car accident in Atlanta, Georgia.

Skip Day of 1940 produced memories for all involved. The only blemish on a perfect day came later in the month.

At the May PTA meeting, an elderly woman complained that the high school seniors should not have been allowed to attend a movie that had profanity.

Superintendent Smith responded: "Yes, Rhett Butler said to Scarlett O'Hara: 'Frankly, my dear, I don't give a damn!' I am sure these 18 year-olds have heard worse swearing in their days." With that, the meeting was declared adjourned and lunch was served.

The Wentworth class of 1940 believed that they had the best skip day ever. Other classes thought their experience was the best too. The truth is, life only gives high school seniors one Skip Day but the memories last a lifetime.

So What Happened to the Skip Day Money?

There is no exact record of the balance of the 1940 Senior Skip Day money left in the Dakota State Bank. It would have been less than $20. The money remained in the bank at 3% yearly interest year after year.

The seniors all graduated and said goodbye to high school. In 1942, Superintendent Smith moved. No one felt a responsibility to check on the money, however the Harringtons, owners of the bank, secured it for 60 years.

The Wentworth school closed in 1966 and the students were sent to a nearby school district. Celeste Harrington, also an owner of the bank, had been an English teacher for the class of 1940 in their freshman year. When the school building burned down and the land was sold, Celeste provided money for the school bell to be located in the City Park which is a part of the business area.

In 1999, the Harrington family sold the Dakota State Bank and the account was brought to the attention of school alumni. By the year 2000, the 1940 Senior Skip Day account had grown to approximately $280.00.

Memorial Day always has been a day for a military service at the local cemetery followed by a meal served at the Legion Hall. With money to be used for a special purpose, the three living members of the 1940 class, former teachers and alumni decided to have the last Wentworth School Reunion celebration on Memorial Day 2000.

Celeste Harrington gave her consent to the dedication committee to have the bell and its tower moved back to the school area and placed as a memorial. The bell had been purchased in 1909 and weighed 1,100 pounds. It was trucked back to the former school grounds. The site included a metal stand for the bell and a large tombstone with a photo of the building engraved on the front, Date: 1885-1966.

More than 2000 alumni and friends attended the reunion program held in the Legion Hall during the afternoon and the meal served at the conclusion. The oldest alumnus to attend was 102 years old.

With additional money from alumni and the 1940 class money, bills were paid and the remaining money was donated. $200 was given to the Wentworth Legion Association, $50 for use of the Legion Hall and to the owner of the school property where the bell is erected, $100 for a permanent easement.

Many people worked to make this historic event possible. The bell will be a perpetual memorial for all students who attended the Wentworth Public School, thanks in part to the class of 1940.

Friday the 13th Cookie Caper

A colorful green and white sign was securely fastened to the fence beside the mailbox.

The sign depicted a big green four-leaf clover, the 4-H symbol, plus a message in bold lettering "4-H MEMBERS LIVE HERE." A casual passerby would not know the upcoming frustration of the 13-year old 4-H member, Rebecca, who lived in the white wooden farmhouse behind the tall evergreen trees.

The day was August 13th...Friday, the 13th. Rebecca awoke as the hot August sun streamed through her window creating sparkling flecks on her face. She became aware of the sunlight and then nestled down in the mattress to contemplate what the day had in store for her. This was a special day and time of year, which she looked forward to for twelve long months. It was 4-H Achievement Days at the County Fair.

It was a prelude to the State Fair. It was the time when all rural and some town youth displayed their yearly accomplishments. The rewards were ribbons and the honor to take their winning exhibits to the State Fair.

Rebecca lay in bed thinking that today she must enroll her oatmeal raisin cookies, her stamp collection and yearling calf at the exhibit buildings by 11:00 A.M.

Before leaving the security of her bed, she let her mind drift back to last year's exhibits. Then she was only 12-years old but had received a second place blue ribbon on her special cookies. In her mind, she had not seen any difference between her plate of cookies and the purple ribbon winner. She vowed to get a purple ribbon on her cookies at this year's fair.

Rebecca knew her best chance to win a purple ribbon would be in the cooking category. Her calf was nice but she didn't see it as a champion. Some kids had stamp collections which contained stamps their grandparents had saved so she didn't plan for honors in that exhibit but she was "going for the purple" in the cookie competition.

Her mother was well aware of her ambition, for Rebecca had spent many afternoons baking oatmeal cookies in an attempt at perfection. She had tried many recipes. She had researched her mother's recipe cards, her grandmother's tattered file and many cookbooks. Each time she baked, she experimented with a different recipe. She had fed cookies to her parents, the hired man and her brothers, Tom and Toby. Tom was 16 and could get rid of lots of them but Toby, age 7, wasn't too keen on her concoctions. He mostly played with his cookies or fed them to "Silver" the cat. The hired man came into the kitchen for morning and afternoon coffee and was her best taste tester. He always told her the cookies were perfect.

Toward the end of the summer, only the hired man was eating her "taste" cookies. He usually dipped them into his coffee and then ate them. Rebecca kept changing her recipes and ingredients to find the winning combination.

One really warm Saturday morning she tried a recipe her grandmother had found in an old church cookbook. She stirred it up, carefully made the little mounds on the cookie sheets and guarded them while they baked. She took them out of the oven to find beautiful, browned cookies; no burned raisins sticking through the top. There were no crisp edges or depressed centers. She broke one in half and tasted it. She decided this was her perfect batch. After they cooled, her mother helped her pick out thirteen perfect cookies. She carefully packed them into a 3-lb coffee can between little squares of waxed paper and put them into the basement freezer to await the County Fair.

The rules were clear on the information sheet sent out by the County Home Extension Agent. Class A: Oatmeal Raisin Cookies: Place twelve cookies on a paper plate with wax paper and tape a cookie to the top of the plate along with your name, 4-H club and address. The top cookie was for the judge to taste-test. So, thirteen cookies were needed for the entry.

Rebecca finally ended her daydreaming and bounded out of bed. She went into the kitchen where her mother was already busy cooking for the men who would be coming in for dinner, the big noontime meal. Tom was eating his breakfast and he would later take her to town since they both had exhibits to enter. He would load the truck with Rebecca's calf and his own livestock entries and she would ride in the cab. She could hold her cookies and stamp collection on her lap.

Before eating her cereal, Rebecca raced to the basement to take her cookies out of the freezer to thaw. She carefully unpacked them onto a tray on the dining room table. They looked as beautiful as when she had frozen them. She stood back to admire them and then began to count...1, 2, 3, and finally reached 12. There were no more! She counted again. The number was 12. She called her mother to count and she also counted 12. She looked into the bottom of the can. No more cookies. One cookie was gone! Who took it? Who ate it? Toby kept playing with the cat and said he didn't eat those kinds of cookies. Of course Mother was innocent and Tom said he didn't remember taking any cookies out of the freezer cans. Dad never messed around with things in the kitchen, and he only ate the food set in front of him.

They all counted and again the number of cookies was 12. Rebecca looked at the clock and sniffled that she would have to make more cookies to qualify the entry. Mother was baking a roast in the oven but said she'd finish it on the top burner while Rebecca baked another batch of cookies.

The stress and tension in the kitchen took all the fun out of the project. She re-read the recipe, mixed the dough, greased the pans and dropped the cookies. She carefully watched the baking between bites of breakfast. She took the cookies out in fifteen minutes and then put them back a little longer to brown. She finally decided they were done. She almost cried as she looked over the batch. There weren't thirteen symmetrical cookies on the pan. None of them looked like her frozen batch so she couldn't substitute one for the missing cookie. Her mother observed, "A recipe never turns out exactly the same way twice."

It was 10:00 A.M. when Tom came from the barn wanting to know how soon she would be ready. He had loaded the livestock and would change clothes and be ready to leave for town. Becky felt like a deflated balloon. How could she possibly enter these cookies? They were not perfect. Tears hung in her eyes but her mother consoled her with the fact that she had done her best and she had better quit feeling bad and get ready to take the entries to the fair.

She changed her clothes and gathered her stamp collection and the thirteen not-so-perfect cookies. All the while she was feeling vengeance for the person who had stolen and eaten the one important cookie. "I hope he got sick!" she lamented.

As Rebecca rode over the gravel road in the truck cab, holding her plate of cookies, she quizzed Tom if he remembered eating the cookie. He said he had better things to do this summer than sneak around stealing cookies out of the freezer. Anyway, he was tired of oatmeal cookies. He said if they had been chocolate chips she could have considered him the culprit.

She stood in line at the County Extension Building to enter her cookies but her excitement and enthusiasm were gone, as she did not think her entry was of prize-winning caliber. Rebecca registered them at the proper place along with her stamp collection, and then went with Tom to enroll her calf. She met some friends in whom she confided her tale of woe. They reminded her that Friday the 13th was usually unlucky. She didn't tell them how hard she had worked all summer and how badly she wanted to win the purple ribbon at the County Fair.

Rebecca spent the next hours with her friends. They viewed all the livestock pens, petted the rabbits and watched men set up the carnival. She ate hotdogs, drank pop and visited with school friends. She watched the foot races while her mind was on the judges who were tasting and rating the foods in the homemakers' building. By 4:00 P.M. the exhibits had been judged and the public was allowed to view them. Rebecca's heart was heavy as she walked to the cookie exhibit. A blue ribbon again this year! A girl from the Pleasant Valley 4-H Club had won the purple ribbon.

As her friends gathered around her, Rebecca decided to remember her 4-H ideals of good sportsmanship and enjoy the rest of the day. She knew that next year's 4-H Achievement Days would not fall on the 13th.

After the final grandstand act, Rebecca climbed into the family truck with her brother for the ride home. Just as they were backing the big red truck, George Phillips, Tom's friend, stuck his head into the window to visit with Tom. George noticed Rebecca and looked her straight in the eye. She felt a pang of excitement as he had never paid attention to her. She had always hoped he would notice her and not think of her as Tom's kid sister.

George asked Rebecca, "Hey, what did you get on your cookies?" She confessed shyly, "I got just a blue ribbon again." George grinned and said, "Gee, that's too bad! You should have had purple! I sneaked one of your goodies out of the freezer last week when Tom and I were working on our scrapbooks. They were terrific! I thought you had a purple winner for sure!"

Rebecca's heart gave a little flip and she smiled back. It was worth it to have George notice her. She lost the purple ribbon but gained an admirer. A pretty "fair" result after all.

Sailor Daddy

"'Sailor Daddy' will be home soon!" These were the words Ronnie was waiting to hear.

Jim Johnson was en route home from his duty on the USS Yosemite, a destroyer tender which was anchored for three months in the Japanese Harbor after WWII ended. The sailors on the USS Yosemite were trained to repair United States naval ships which had been damaged during the war. The ship had been sent to Sasebo Bay, Japan, between Nagasaki and Hiroshima after the final bombs ending the war had been dropped. The crew on the USS Yosemite worked feverishly repairing damaged ships so they could make it across the Pacific Ocean and enjoy a hero's welcome.

The USS Yosemite had an entertainment band on board, which served to provide music for the sailors. The band was available for their shipmates and to entertain servicemen in areas where they were stationed. It was December 11, 1945 when the USS Yosemite band members got orders to return to the United States and be discharged from their wartime service.

Jim was one of the band members who lived in South Dakota. He was anxious to return home for Christmas and had hopes of pheasant hunting before the season was over. What Jim didn't know was that the pheasant hunting had been extended that year so returning servicemen could enjoy the "world's best" pheasant hunting.

Ronnie had seen pictures of his father in Navy white uniform. He called him my "Sailor Daddy". Ronnie was only two years old when his father joined the Navy. He was anxious to see him. "Will Daddy know me?" Ronnie asked. "I want to see him!"

Jim was fortunate to arrive in the United States on December 22nd. A troop train had sent him from San Francisco to Fort Snelling Military Station in St. Paul, Minnesota, where he had enlisted two years previously. He had been assigned to the USS Yosemite band because of his special skills and his Masters Degree in music. Jim was coming home without injury or disease, unlike many other Veterans.

When arriving at Fort Snelling, there were few telephones available for the servicemen to call their families to tell them they were back in the United States and waiting to get back home.

Telephone operators were trained not to talk to people on the party telephone line unless it was to notify residents of a problem such as a death, bad weather, chicken theives, gypsies, or fires in the area. However, the local operator, Mrs. Harvey, recognized the telephone call made for the Johnson family and she knew they were not home.

They had not been answering their party line of one long and two short rings. She decided that this was an emergency so she spoke to Jim and told him that his parents were probably playing cards at the Fisher home as they often did on Saturday nights. She told Jim to hang on the phone and she would dial the Fisher's to see if his parents were there.

Jim stayed on the line and prayed that his parents were at the Fisher's so he could tell them to pick him up at the bus depot at 7:00 A.M. the next morning. His father was at the Fisher's and got the telephone operator's message that Jim was on the line. Jim's father could hardly think of anything to say except, "I'll be there!"

Jim said he couldn't talk anymore as the bus was waiting for him to go to Sioux City, Iowa, which would take until morning. He hung up so others could use the phone.

"We'll be sure that the war is over when Jim gets home," his father said. The people "rubbering" on the telephone line agreed.

It was the "dead of winter" in the northern states as there was a lot of snow. Most of the country roads were only open in one lane but Jim's father was used to icy and snowy roads. He decided to leave very early so he could be in Sioux City when the bus came in from St. Paul. He drove his two seated home-modified La Fayette half car/half truck.

He also knew that Jim would not have warm clothes to wear. So he brought extra blankets and some food for Jim to eat, as he doubted there would be a place to buy food when traveling all night on a bus. His dad also took a big shovel and pair of Jim's old overshoes. It was 30 miles each way to bring Jim home. He also hoped that the bus depot would be open so the servicemen could be warm while they waited to be picked up for their final trip home.

As it was night the bus that was taking the servicemen from St. Paul to their destinations in Minnesota and Iowa stopped only for gas. One of the gas stations had an outhouse in the back of the building and some pop and candy to purchase. These were appreciated by the servicemen who had waited for their trip home for a long time. They were happy that they were coming home in good health and had survived through their years in the terrible war.

They tried to sleep on the bus but it was crowded yet none of them complained. The war was over. They were headed home. In fact, the bus was filled with stories, one trying to outdo the other.

The Johnson family worried about Dad driving to Sioux City in the night to bring Jim back from the bus depot. He would be alone on the road until 7:00 A.M. Grandma Gertrude said that she wouldn't be able to sleep until they heard from Dad that they were safe in Sioux City. Ronnie was four-years old and he was as concerned as the rest of the family. By 4:00 A.M. Jim's dad was on the road in order to be at the bus depot by 7:00 A.M. and bring "Sailor Daddy" home.

Ronnie had been sitting on his mom, Mary's, lap trying to stay awake. He hugged and patted his dog, Laddie. The news of Daddy coming home was a huge event causing excitement like Ronnie had never felt before... even bigger than the town celebration when it was announced the war was over.

"I'll make some popcorn and time will go faster." I'll see if we can get WNAX on the radio as they are usually on most of the night," Grandma said. "We can try to take a little nap." she added. "If Jim comes into Sioux City at 7:00 A.M., it will probably be almost 10:00 A.M. when they get home." Then she said, "I hope he calls home when the bus comes in. Then we will know how much longer we will have to wait!"

The family was napping and Ronnie was sound asleep when the phone rang a little before 7:00 A.M. Since most of the people on the party line knew that Jim was en route home, they picked up their telephones to listen to what time he would return home after two years in the U.S. Navy.

Jim was on the phone and said that the trip to Sioux City went well and as soon as his luggage was unloaded from the bus, he and Dad would be on the road home! People on the party telephone line were listening as Jim was talking. When he left the telephone, the neighbors and friends were fast at telling the Johnsons how happy they were for them. They said they would be glad to see Jim in church on Sunday. It was a familiar story in 1945 as a community would learn when one of their "native sons" was coming home from the war.

After the Johnsons hung up the telephone, it began to ring constantly with even more friends and neighbors calling to tell Gertrude and Mary how glad they were that Jim would be home for Christmas. They all hoped to see him and visit during Christmas and New Years. News traveled fast from the party phone line through the town "grapevine."

The Johnsons announced that they would have a party at the church after Christmas so everyone could visit with Jim and the family.

"What will Ronnie think when he sees his 'Sailor Daddy'?" several asked.

Ronnie was up and watching out the window when the car drove into the yard. He yelled at everyone and started for the door when his mother caught him because it was cold and slippery outside but he got away and ran without a hat or coat to see his daddy!

After they hugged and kissed, the family helped him unload the car with the many boxes and seabag full of treasures that Jim had brought home! The family finally sat down to eat dinner. Ronnie hardly took his eyes off his father. He was having great difficulty talking to his father since nearly everyone was talking at once.

Ronnie finally blurted out, "Did they call you 'Sailor Daddy' in the Navy?" "No," his father said. "I am just plain 'Daddy' to you from now on and I will never leave you again!"

Ronnie thought for a minute and replied, "Alright, 'Plain Daddy'. Thanks for coming home and saying goodbye to 'Sailor Daddy.'"

By the time the family had supper, they were all exhausted from lack of sleep and the excitement of the day. But they sat in the living room as happy as a family could be as World War II was over and Jim was safely home. Ronnie said he was not going to let his daddy leave him again.

Ronnie sat on his father's lap until he fell asleep. His mother carefully had Jim put him in bed and cover him up without taking off his clothes since that might wake him up. They knew Ronnie needed sleep with Christmas coming in just two days.

When Ronnie was put in his bed, their dog Laddie lay on a rug beside his bed. Laddie seemed to know that the day had been an exciting one.

The next day Ronnie was up early. He went into his parents' bedroom. "Hey, 'Plain Daddy,' get up. You had all that time to sleep in the Navy. We've got things to do!"

Where's Tweedy Bird!

The early spring sunshine was flooding the kitchen table as Millie placed a plate of fried eggs and bacon in front of her husband, Walter. Now was the time to talk about her desire for a new wall to wall carpet, Millie decided. Walter was happy as he glanced at the morning paper. He buttered toast and gave a few crumbs to Tweedy, the family parakeet perched on his shoulder. Tweedy pecked at the crumbs and hopped on the table wanting more crumbs. Walter smiled and put more crumbs on the table for the bird.

Under ordinary circumstances, Millie would have protested having the bird on the table but she was willing to indulge her husband while she brought up "The Subject."

"Walt," she said, keeping her tone of voice soft and sweet, "I'd really like to buy new wall to wall living room carpet."

Walt's attention quickly focused from Tweedy to his wife whom he called Mildred in formal circumstances. "What is wrong with the rug we have?" was his startled reply.

Without hesitation, Millie launched into her prepared sales pitch. "It's because we've had the same rug for SIXTEEN YEARS! It's faded and old-fashioned. It's worn out. Look how it's tramped down around the birdcage where everyone stands to feed and talk to

Tweedy. I want to redecorate and new wall to wall carpet comes first."

"But Mildred," Walter protested, "you are talking about a BIG job. We'd have to take up the old rug and have a new one put down. It's a job to move all the furniture."

"We do it every spring when we put this old rug on the clothes line and beat it with carpet beaters. Our carpet beaters are even worn out!" she told him.

Millie quickly continued, "I've talked to friends and it isn't bad at all. The carpet layers will do all the work. All we have to do is pick out the carpet we want. It's as simple as that!"

". . .And PAY for it," interjected the surprised husband.

"Besides that," she continued, "this is 1950! Remember we'll be celebrating our 25th wedding anniversary in September and people will be visiting us. Our children and grandkids will come to celebrate with us. We don't want our home to look shabby!"

"The old rug sure looks good to me. Are you sure we need a new rug? Can you buy this same pattern again?" Walt asked.

"I'd like something different." Millie explained, "I'm tired of the same old flowery patterns. They don't even sell these kinds of rugs anymore. Carpets are now installed to fit the whole room and it can't be pulled up!"

Walt couldn't think of another thing to say except, "Gee, well, I didn't know you felt that this was so important. Go ahead and pick something out. I have coffee every morning with Pete from the furniture store. Maybe he has something we can put down."

Millie wasn't through with her sales talk. "Walter! I want a GOOD carpet! We'll probably have the new carpet for the rest of our lives. I'd like to look at all the new wall to wall patterns," she said.

"Well, look where you want," conceded the puzzled husband, "but watch the checkbook."

With that Walter put Tweedy in the birdcage, patted the bird's head and walked into the garden to think about his wife's shopping expedition.

By the dinner hour, Millie had made the rounds of all the stores selling carpet in the area. The backseat of the car was loaded with huge books of carpet pictures and pieces of carpet samples. She recruited Walt to help her unload them.

Millie chattered through dinner about grades of pad, kinds of fiber, statistics on wear and the yardage estimated. Walt sat with glassy eyes and fed crumbs to Tweedy. He was aware that she made no mention of price.

After dinner, Millie spread the samples out on the living room floor and insisted that Walt look at them. He protested by saying that the household was her department. He was as interested in the carpet as she would have been if he had asked her to examine the engine of the car.

"Pick what you want," he said. "Just don't buy one of those ugly ones like mother used to have with ferns in the rug pattern."

"Walt!" Millie exclaimed. "They don't even make fern patterned carpet anymore!"

"Well," he looked at a sample on top and said, "how about this orange one?"

"Walt!" she almost cried. "It wouldn't match anything in this house!"

"Pick out what you want, but do you remember how allergic you were to the new carpet at church? You don't want to get sick, do you? We can't move the heavy furniture like the piano and buffet and take up the old carpet without help, you know." With that added protest, Walt had no more to say. He took the newspaper and Tweedy into the den and turned on the radio to listen to "The Jack Benny Show."

Millie was humming a tune the next evening and reported to her husband, "It's all picked out! The nice man at the store came out to measure our room. He says we need about 60 yards in order to match the seams. They will put down the best pad and the new wall to wall carpet. We can have it installed in about 10 days, as they have to special order it."

"What about moving the furniture?" was Walt's latest worry.

"Oh, that's the good part," his spouse explained. "Larry the Layer is very experienced at all of this. He will have help to take out the furniture and the old carpet, lay the new one and put back the furniture all in one day. All we have to do is pick up the small things the night before. Can you believe that?"

"No," Walt thought, "I'll believe it when the job is done and I pay the bill."

A phone call the following week alerted Walt and Millie that the new wall to wall carpet arrived and would be laid the next day.

The night before the living room transformation was to take place, Millie enlisted Walt's help in moving end tables, magazine racks, knickknacks and lamps while she packed dishes from the hutch and put them into boxes. "These all need washing and dusting, anyway," she reminded herself.

"Do I have to stay home and help tomorrow?" asked Walt.

"No, I asked him that and do you know what he told me? He said, 'I charge $1.00 a yard for laying carpet and a dollar a yard extra if the husband stays home to help.'" Walt did not think that was funny.

"What about Tweedy tomorrow? We can't have him in the way. He likes to fly in and out of his cage."

"I've already thought of your bird." Millie explained, "We'll put his cage in the den and he can fly in and out all day without a problem. I'm going to have lunch with Dorothy and Ethel and then we are going to the afternoon matinee at the Granada Theater. The show will be *The Farmer's Daughter* as none of us saw it when it played here several years ago. Actress Loretta Young is a favorite of mine. Charles Bickford is the actor but I've never seen him in a show. It should be good!"

"You can mow the back lawn in the morning, go to Kiwanis at noon and go fishing in the afternoon. That way we'll be out of Larry's way and when we come home late afternoon, the place will look like new. Maybe we had better plan to eat dinner out tomorrow night in case I'm allergic to the new carpet smell. See how simple this will be?"

Walt did not reply.

The next morning at 8:00 A.M. when the couple was finishing breakfast, a truck pulled into their driveway. Walt and Millie looked out the window, took another gulp from their coffee cups and read the sign on the truck:

LARRY THE LAYER
HAPPY CARPET DAYS!

Walt jumped up to open the back door and tipped his coffee over the kitchen table! He said, "Darn it!" A big roll of carpet protruded from the back of the vehicle and a smaller roll of white padding was being unloaded by two men.

Walt took a look at the color of the new carpet as it was being placed on the back porch. He could only see the end of the roll but he remarked, "Gosh, that's the same color as Tweedy . . .blue and greenish. We'll never find him if he is in the living room! You sure found a color to match everything," was Walt's curt remark.

The men went right to work, declining Millie's offer of coffee and rolls. They began moving the big pieces of furniture into rooms adjacent to the living room. They assured the couple that they could return after 4:00 P.M. and the job would be completed.

Millie remarked how nice it was for them to move the big furniture and Larry said, "Oh, we really are furniture movers but we lay a little carpet on the side." Walt didn't think that was funny either.

The couple changed their clothes and left through the front door. They silently realized that their home was now in the possession of two strange men who were wrestling with big pieces of carpet. They weren't sure they should leave for the day.

By late afternoon, the carpet job was nearing completion so Larry sent his assistant back to the store to check on a job for the following day. Larry finished the door metals and stood up to survey the job. He reached into his shirt picket for his package of cigarettes and found it empty. He then looked across the floor to see where he dropped them only to discover a small hump in the carpet. The little mound was where the piano would be sitting. It dawned on him that the cigarettes must have fallen out of his pocket and under the pad when the carpet was rolled out.

Larry thought a minute and decided, "I'll just mash it down and no one will be the wiser. He took the mallet from his toolbox and gave the little hump a couple blows and battered it flat. "There," he thought. "No one will ever know the difference." His assistant came in and they put the furniture in place and the job was done. He told Harry to leave and that he'd meet him at the office in the morning for their next job.

He gathered up the tool chests and took them to the truck. As he opened the door, he noticed his package of cigarettes lying on the front seat. They were not the hump under the carpet!

Within minutes Millie drove up, put her packages on the kitchen table and glanced in the living room to see the new carpet. Larry got out of his truck and told her, "I'm glad you like it. We'll mail the bill." He left as fast as he could.

At the same time, Walt parked his car in the front of the house and came into the living room. He looked at the new carpet and beautiful room. He skipped across the room where Millie was standing in admiration. He put his arm around her and gave her a hug. Then he kissed her and said, ""Honey, I'm sorry I gave you such a bad time with this carpet deal. You deserve another kiss."

They were heading for the kitchen for some coffee when Walt said, "Where is Tweedy Bird?" They found his cage door open and no bird. "Tweedy Bird," they called. They frantically searched the house! The search continued for days. But Tweedy Bird was never found!

How Time Flies

Modern bridal showers continue a great tradition, not only for the bride, but also neighbors, friends, grandparents and mothers. They enjoy giving gifts, seeing what the bride-to-be receives and talking about the anticipated wedding. Older women enjoy sharing stories about the gifts given for their weddings and showers—basic things that were different from today's presents.

As the bride opens her gifts and passes them around the room, the older women will often comment on the differences now from their bridal showers. They recall gifts that they received including heavy pots and pans, recipe books, embroidered aprons, tablecloths and linen napkins. They will comment to each other, "We need new things like this! Maybe we should throw out our old stuff and start over." However, they wouldn't dream of throwing out their old recipe books or faithful frying pans.

The new bride's shower gifts are usually various sizes of pizza pans, quick and easy recipe books, lovely place mats, electric coffee makers and microwave dishes, plus unusual table decorations and fancy dishes.

Often missing at these gatherings is one essential item — the fly swatter. They were mandatory for brides years ago. Women from past generations had one common enemy in their kitchens, the filthy, pesky, ugly flies! The smell of food attracted flies into kitchens and back porches. The only way to beat the beastly insect was to kill him! Every family needed several fly swatters, all at strategic locations to fight the war on flies!

By the 1940's, the heyday of premium giving, as the way of advertising local businesses, the fly swatter from a local merchant became a welcomed gift for the new bride. The swatter often had advertising on the handle or around the top as a way of promoting a business. "If you didn't get a fly swatter, you got a wooden yardstick with the business advertising on it," Maude Tillman insisted.

It was necessary to have swatters made of porous material as the breeze from the solid pieces would not work and the fly usually escaped. Many a youngster earned candy money by killing a given number of flies in their home, most importantly at canning and farm threshing times.

Modern fly swatters have taken on a decorative look ... lightweight, colorful plastic, sometimes decorated with fabric with pictures of butterflies, flowers or other fancy decorations. The old ones were made of a fine mesh screen on a wire handle.

Anyone wanting to revisit the days of flies can still stop by a garbage dump, seed lot, outside garbage pail or picnic area. They are alive and well in droves "or hoards" along with their cousins the wasps, gnats and mosquitoes.

Cooking and cookbooks have become so specialized that the next hot title might be "Cooking Without Flies".

Because some things never totally change, when it comes to keeping house, this small ode of yesterday should be saved for today.

Ode to the Fly Swatter

"Oh Little Fly upon the wall, you are not welcome there at all.

You buzzed around me at sunrise. I will make quick work of your demise!

WHAM! ... The swatter strikes again!"

And for new brides of yesteryear or today: A fly swatter is still a handy tool.

The Kamikaze Pheasant

"HURRAH! THE WAR IS OVER!" was the message on the envelope from Elden who had been in the South Pacific for over two years fighting the Japanese. The letter was dated September 2, 1945, marking the end of World War II.

The letter contained a list of expectations and plans for the future upon his discharge. A note was scribbled on the bottom: "I hope the pheasant season is still on when I get home! I am starving for some good meat. We had Spam over 200 days this year. Please do NOT buy any Spam—ever!"

Wives, children, going back to work and pheasant hunting were on the minds of many Midwest World War II Veterans.

Elden was a South Dakota native where pheasant hunting was part of the world sportsman's paradise. The South Dakota State Bird was the Chinese Ringneck Pheasant. Millions of pheasant hatched each year so they could be hunted in the fall.

For several reasons, the South Dakota 1945 Pheasant Season was extended into January 1946. Two of which were the abundance of pheasants and the extended season would allow returning servicemen a chance to hunt.

On December 23, 1945, Elden was discharged returning home for Christmas and a huge family reunion. The day after Christmas, Elden oiled his model 12-gauge shotgun and bought a hunting license.

The day was blustery, cold, and windy but he convinced his mother-in-law, Rosella, who had a car, to take him hunting for pheasants. The 1939 Plymouth did not have much heat. But since cars were scarce after World War II, anything that would run was good for hunting. Elden promised pheasant meat for supper for the whole family.

Rosella drove, Elden sat in the passenger's seat with his shotgun. His wife was the "spotter" watching for game out the windows. They drove the few blocks out of town toward Highway #34.

Just on the very edge of town, a pheasant was flushed out of the ditch and took to the air. All shouted, "Pheasant!"

Rosella slammed on the brakes; Elden opened the car door, nearly losing his balance as he cocked his gun to shoot. Before he could pull the trigger, a big pheasant rooster lay dead at his feet. Not one shot was fired!

The bird had flown into the city electric wire which was strung across the highway. It crashed into the line, broke his neck and fell to the ground dead. After fighting the Japanese for two years and waiting everyday to bag a South Dakota Pheasant, the pheasant killed himself!

He fortunately shot two more pheasants.

That evening the family enjoyed fried pheasant and mashed potatoes with pheasant gravy—a feast for a returned sailor. They ate by lamplight as the broken wire had put the whole town out of electricity.

Elden could keep guests spellbound for years telling stories from the South Pacific in World War II and the "kamikaze" pheasant that greeted his return.

A Code on the Party Line

The big, wooden telephone hanging on the living room wall was ringing loudly, one long, three short and another long! That was the telephone operator's code for the Larson's telephone ring. With six families on the party telephone line, each had a different group of rings. The telephone line was usually busy.

If people talked too long on the party line or the line was needed for an important reason, the telephone operator told people to hang up. People often hung up their phone and then picked up their phone again to listen to others talking. This was called "rubbering."

When people talked on the party line, they were aware numerous others were listening to their conversation. People who "rubbered" often repeated what they heard on the party line — feeding the local gossip. This was not courteous but it was a way of communication in the days of the party telephone line.

When Olga Larson heard the ring, she yelled at her daughter, Helen, to answer it. "Hello," Helen said. "Mother is making bread but she will be here in a few minutes so you can talk to her."

"Don't bother her." Just tell your mother that I got a bad code so we can't come to visit your family on Sunday!" Helen hung up and the others who were rubbering on the line, clicked off their phones at the same time.

"The Klines aren't coming to visit us on Sunday," Helen told her mother. "Elsie said they aren't coming; something about a code. She hung up right away or I would have told her about a code I'm learning. We are practicing the Morse Code at school. The depot agents use it all the time. They report where the trains are going, whether they are on time and estimated unloading time."

Mother replied, "Was Elsie coughing? "I heard someone coughing when you answered the telephone."

"I think she was coughing".

"Well, I'll bet Elsie was saying she had a 'cold' not a 'code!' I am glad they aren't coming. We don't want to catch a spring cold because they are the worst."

"Lots of kids and the teachers are sneezing and coughing. Our teachers make us cover our mouth when we cough. I am glad we can't catch it on the telephone or we would all be sick!" Helen added.

"Well, we'll have fresh bread and maybe you can find time to make some molasses cookies for our Sunday treat." Mother replied.

"We'll have the boys bring in another basket of cobs for the kitchen stove and I'll find time to make the cookies for Sunday dinner," Mom said.

This sounded better to Helen than listening to the party line with everyone complaining about the cold winter and illnesses which had become popular topics of conversation on the party telephone line.

Sunday came and the family went to church. Just as they came home, the Klines pulled up.

"I thought you were home with a cold," Helen said.

"No, I was trying to talk to you about getting a code so everyone 'rubbering' on the telephone wouldn't know what we were planning!"

Well, come on in and help make lunch. From now on, our telephone code to get together will be "I think I've got a cold!"

A Good Day for Grandpa

Grandpa Joe and Grandma Marge were getting ready for bed as the February wind howled around the corner of the house. Grandpa said, "I'm sure glad we sold the farm last year and we don't have to go outside in this weather to milk cows or feed the pigs and horses and you don't have to take care of the chickens."

Grandma Marge agreed. "It is really good to live in town. We can walk to the grocery store and church. We can drive to nearby towns to see a movie on Sunday nights. It was time you retired after working so hard all of your life. You didn't have to buy one of those expensive tractors farmers think they need now either."

"The kids have better jobs than farming during these dust bowl days. Betty likes teaching country school and Jackie has a good job delivering mail in town. The grand kids like living in town, too."

"Tell you what," Joe declared. "We've had a busy week. Let's just sleep late in the morning. Saturday is a good day to catch a few extra winks. That's what retirement is all about." Marge settled deeper into the soft mattress and pulled the heavy comforter over the top. "We're just like the kids used to be on the 'no school tomorrow' days when the weather was bad!" She giggled as she drifted off to dream of their happy retirement.

At 7:00 A.M., their dreamland was invaded by the sharp "beep-beep-beep" of their alarm clock. "I forgot to shut the darn thing off last night!" He stumbled over to the radio and an announcer was reporting, ". . .registers twenty degrees below zero. It will be a cold one today!"

Almost simultaneously the telephone rang, bringing Joe to his feet and a run across the cold floor to the kitchen telephone. Marge lay in the warm bed and wondered, "What now?"

Joe returned to the bedroom shivering as he reported, "That was Pete. He wants to pick me up in an hour to go ice fishing at Lake Campbell. He has a friend who has offered us his icehouse for the day. He says the fish are really biting."

Marge was wide-awake and shivering, too. "You must be out of your mind!"

"We'll find some." Joe grinned like a schoolboy. "I'm going fishing! I've always wanted to go ice fishing and today is that day!"

Marge jumped out of bed, wrapped her heavy bathrobe around her, and dashed to the kitchen. She lit her new kerosene stove and filled the coffeepot with water and an egg-coffee mixture and another pan of water with oatmeal. "You can't eat enough hot food on a cold day like this," shaking her head in disbelief regarding her husband's anticipated adventure.

Joe hadn't ice fished in years. Summer fishing was another story. He bought a fishing license each spring so that he could fish from shore during the summertime. But ice fishing sounded like going to the end of the world as far as she was concerned.

Joe was all smiles when he came into the kitchen, wearing his bathrobe and asked, "What shall I wear?"

"Heaven only knows!" was Marge's reply.

80

Together they went into the basement. Joe put a couple shovels of coal into the furnace and saw Marge pulling out a box of old hunting clothes left by their son who had grown up and left home years before. She pulled out a pair of heavy gray boot socks, the kind with a red stripe around the top and a red toe. "You can wear these with your overshoes!"

"I don't think they will fit in my shoes," Joe murmured. "Well, they'll HAVE to," Marge replied. Next came an old pair of tan-colored hunting pants. "You can wear these over your work trousers and "this" pulling out an old blue stocking cap . . .and take Jackie's letterman's sweater. It is good and heavy."

By now the coffee was perking and the oatmeal was boiling over the pan onto the stove. Marge said some words, " . . .Heck! . . .Darn!" She thought of a few other descriptive words.

Joe sensed her frustrations and tried to soothe her with, "I'm not going to the Arctic! I'll be in Pete's truck and then there is a stove in the icehouse. Pete says he'd bring bait and lunch. Do you know where my tackle box is stored?"

"If I'd known last night," she fumed, "I'd have made some stuff for your lunch. Are you SURE you want to go?"

Joe was sure!

After Joe ate breakfast in record time, he went to find his tackle box which was behind the furnace. Marge made another trip to the basement and returned with a moth-eaten scarf and some old gloves that had survived a long-ago hunting trip. She added these to the pile of fishing clothes.

A horn honked and Pete was in the driveway to pick up his fishing companion. Marge pressed a sack of fruit, apples and bananas, from the dining room fruit bowl into her husband's hands as he went out the door with a pile of clothing.

The pickup truck, with two fishermen, disappeared in a cloud of whirling snow heading into a cold north wind.

Marge peered through the frosted window and a wave of nostalgia swept over her. "He's like a kid going to the circus." She said to no one. She remembered how he loved being out-of-doors in his younger days and how much hunting and fishing meant to him.

Marge sat by the kitchen table and nibbled on some toast. She then downed two cups of coffee. "Well," she reasoned, almost aloud, "He'll die happy." She spent the rest of the morning calling friends, mending and pressing clothes, cooking and cleaning. She needed to keep busy.

At noon the phone rang and she nearly jumped out of her skin! "Pa's in trouble!" she declared. But the call was from their grandson Terry who lived in Chicago. He wanted to know if they were okay. He said they were having a terrible blizzard in their area. The radio was talking about closing O'Hare airport. When his grandma told him about his grandpa's fishing trip, he couldn't believe it. "He must be crazy to go on a day like this! Why did you let him go?" She tried to explain that there is heat in fish houses and his determination to go. Terry listened and agreed, "When Grandpa makes up his mind, you might as well let him go. I'll tell this story to the guys at coffee Monday. They'll think that my Prairie Grandpa is some kind of Eskimo but they'll be impressed. Keep in touch! Love ya!"

It was nearly dusk when she heard the old pickup rattle to a stop in the driveway. Joe burst in the back door enveloped in a cloud of steam. He was all smiles as he handed her a battered pail containing a skinny, long Northern Pike, still wriggling in water at the bottom of the pail.

"Didn't have a way to clean him," he apologized, grinning from ear-to-ear. "Pete said his wife would skin him if he brought a fish home to clean in the kitchen and for her to cook."

"SIT DOWN!" Marge commanded as she tried to move his dripping overshoes onto a throw rug to keep the kitchen floor dry. "Did you freeze?" She asked.

"Freeze? Land sakes, Marge, I nearly died from sweating. You made me wear so many clothes, I could hardly walk." He started peeling off his heavy clothes while the slimy fish flopped in the pail. Marge gave it a hard look to make sure it was still confined.

"Well first," Joe related, "the truck was acting funny but we found a gas station near the lake. We put a can of deicer in the gas tank. That did the trick. But when we got to the lake, we couldn't find the right fish house. They all looked alike in the snow. Pete had used it last winter but it wasn't in the same spot. We walked and walked but finally found the right number and sure enough, the key fit the lock."

He continued, "There was a propane stove in there and we finally got it lit. We were so hot from walking that we took off our heavy clothes. Pete's old auger was rusty so it took 'till about noon to get the ice holes open and all that stuff. Pete brought some cans of soup to heat on top of the stove. The coffee from his thermos sure went down good! We fished all afternoon but the fish just weren't biting."

"Another guy stopped to visit. He was trying to find his friend's fish house. He was really lost but he moved on after warming up. We tried to dig fish holes outside the shack but the wind was so strong and cold we gave up on that. We sat in the pickup awhile and listened to the radio as we kept checking our lines. We had forgotten about the fruit you sent so the bananas were frozen but we ate the apples after we warmed them over the stove."

"We were ready to give up when that bit. We thought we had a big one 'cuz he put up a real fight. We both worked with him and finally brought him up. He's a dandy. Might weigh 3 pounds or more. We got our pant legs wet and they froze before we left but they thawed out some coming home."

Joe sniffed the air, "I'm starved. Do I smell sauerkraut?"

Marge opened the oven door and pulled out a big roaster of short ribs and kraut with potatoes steaming on the top. Joe dug in and ate like he hadn't had food all winter.

The six o'clock news wasn't over when he was snoring in his big recliner. Just before he fell asleep, he muttered, "That sure was a great fishing trip."

Marge looked at the fish in the pail and the fish looked back. She put a cookie sheet over the top and set it in the back porch until Grandpa could rejuvenate himself enough to clean his catch. She poured another cup of coffee and sighed, "It sure doesn't take much to make some men happy!"

On Sunday, the sun was shining and the wind had died down. It was a very nice winter day. When their friends called to ask to go to a movie, Marge asked Joe and he agreed. They hadn't seen a good movie for some time.

"We'll leave about 1:00 P.M. as the show will start at 3:00. We want to see the new *Mr. Smith Goes to Washington* which will be showing at the Egyptian Theater on Phillips Avenue."

En route, Joe and Marge sat in the backseat. Joe kept laying his head on the seat dozing off. Margie thought he needed the sleep after his fishing extravaganza.

During the show, Joe began to snore and Marge poked him with her elbow. The day on the ice was catching up with him.

He did become interested in the show and raved about it on the way home.

He had cleaned the fish that morning and when they arrived home, they gave their friends some of it to take home and fry.

It had been a very good day for Grandpa. He told their friends "fishing on a bad day beats working on a good day!"

A Bitter Sweet Christmas Eve

Police Sergeant O'Malley was not happy as he sat at his large metal desk and peered at the patterns the street light was making on the snow-covered window of the municipal building which housed the City Jail. It had been his lot to serve duty at the institution on Christmas Eve; the one night he longed to be with his family on the other side of town. He stared absent-mindedly at the little aluminum Christmas tree in the corner of the room. There were no gifts under it and the steady glow of the unblinking blue lights reflected into his glasses.

The telephone rang. O'Malley was jarred from his thoughts to answer, with tension and brusqueness in his voice "City Jail...O'Malley speaking," he responded. "Hi, my dear man," his wife's lilting voice reported, "The children and I are leaving for midnight mass now and should be home by 1:00 A.M. or a little later. I'll check on you then. Hope the night isn't too long. We'll make up for it with a good time playing with the kids tomorrow...love you" and she hung up. He walked to the coffeepot and found it cold. He peered out the window and envisioned his spouse and children seated in church this Christmas Eve...the music, the trees and poinsettias, the smell of incense and pine — the wonder of it all. He could imagine Michael sitting uncomfortably in the pew for fear he was the only boy wearing a white shirt and bow tie. He thought of Sarah feeling proud of her red velvet dress with white bows. How he wished he was seated with them but his job was with the police force and tonight there were men in jail who could not look forward to happiness on Christmas morning. He again sat at his desk. The monitor was silent; the place was quiet and cold. O'Malley shivered a little and picked up the Police Journal to read.

Across the town Karen Weston was sitting at her kitchen table sipping a cup of coffee before cleaning up the array of dishes, wrapping paper and paraphernalia, which represented completed Christmas projects. Tomorrow the little girls would be up early to see what Santa had left under the tree. The family would have to hustle to get to church on time Christmas morning.

Husband Randy was deep in concentration as he began the task of deciphering the "slots A-B and D" to assemble the metal dollhouse for Elizabeth's Santa gift. Elizabeth and her sister, April, were sound asleep. Dad was certain that Elizabeth was dreaming of the wished-for abode to house her precious Barbie dolls. It was nearly 10:30 P.M. and the task looked like another hour or more. "Why do the big gifts always come KD (knocked down)? They don't tell you that when you purchase them at the store," he complained to himself. The boys, Mike and Matt, were watching a Christmas special program on TV. They were enjoying it according to the laughter coming from their room.

Karen had packed boxes of cookies and bars for neighbors and friends. They would finish delivering them after church in the morning. She always baked what her husband called, "a million cookies". She smiled as she remembered her husband's comment of earlier in the week, "She won't let us eat them hot from the oven. They have to be frosted and decorated first, then we have to eat bells and stars until the Fourth of July". She guessed that was true. Tonight her feet hurt but her heart was filled with such joy and rapture of the season that she said a prayer to the Lord for the wonderful message of Christmas. She had written in her Christmas letters, "Christ is the reason for the season."

Karen wished everyone in the world had as much to be thankful for as she felt this night. She envisioned the men in the Penitentiary and wondered if they had holiday treats. She had read of organizations in town who were having programs and distributing goodies to the inmates at the "State Pen", as it was called. Their family had donated food to all the drives, Boy Scouts, Food Pantry, Salvation Army and Social Services. Her thoughts continued, "No one should be lonely or without a sweet treat on this Holy Night."

Suddenly the scene at the City Jail popped into her head. She recalled visiting one of her former foster children who had problems with the law. She remembered how happy he was when she brought him candy bars and coins for the pop machine. He had told her that he was cold but it didn't seem cold to her that day...just barren and unfriendly with ominous bars of confinement.

She grabbed the phone book and found the number listed under "Municipal",

It read simply, City Jail and a number. She dialed the number before she really realized what she was going to say. At the first ring the phone was answered by "City Jail- O'Malley speaking!" Karen's soft, timid voice questioned, "Do you have enough treats for the men in jail tonight?" O'Malley, taken by complete surprise answered, "Naw, there's nothing here. Why?"

"Well," she continued, "if I bring some cookies will you give them to the men?" The Sergeant, now perking up to the idea responded, "Guess so! Why not? The men seem to be awake but it's snowing out there. Are you sure you want to come?" Karen asked, "How many people do you have there tonight?"

O'Malley continued to doodle on the desk pad and quipped, "Well, lets see—ten in the cells and some of the staff here...sure you want to come out on a night like this?" Karen was sure.

There was still a light in her friend's kitchen across the street. She dialed the number. "Merry Christmas!" was the answering reply. "Hey, Rita, do you have a few cookies or bars to spare?" "Sure do! What Salvation Army scheme have you thought of now?" Rita joked.

Karen explained, "I just found out that the men in the City Jail don't have treats tonight. I'm going to take some down there."

"Yet, t-o-n-i-g-h-t?" was the surprised response. "Well, I guess it is Christmas Eve. Sure, I'll help out. In fact, I'll go with you." Rita had become inflamed with the spirit-of-giving by her good friend. "Just give me time to put on some heavy clothes and pack a box of stuff...about 10 minutes or so. I'll watch for you to drive up."

Karen knew her friend, Kathy, was always up late at night. She called with the same message. Kathy thought a minute and replied. You are the answer to a small prayer. Every year Aunt Minnie sends us a butter pecan fruitcake from Georgia. The kids won't touch it. I'm on a diet and Tom's diabetic so the precious cake dies a natural refrigerator death about Valentine's Day. I'll slice it up and put it in a box for you to pick up."

"Wonderful!" was Karen's reply. "I'll be there in about fifteen minutes. I'll just run in and grab it."

Karen located a large white dress box in the basement, lined it with foil and began putting an assortment of cookies and bars into the bottom,

She added a few of her Scandinavian delicacies on the top. "They'll have coffee there," she said to no one. As she put on her coat and informed her husband of the errand, she grabbed a pile of paper napkins from the holder on the kitchen table.

She carefully set the box in the back seat of the car and drove across to Rita's driveway. Rita jumped into the car carrying a like-looking box of treats and explained breathlessly... "Had a couple of extra boxes of chocolate-covered cherries to throw in, too!"

At Kathy's house they barely stopped the car when Kathy came running out the door with her contribution of the fruitcake, "God bless Aunt Minnie and her cake," was Kathy's parting shot.

———————

O'Malley saw the shadow of two women pass the window. Before they could ring the admission bell, he was there to assist them with their packages. "Thanks," he mumbled. "The guys will like, this!" The women put their boxes on the desk, said, "Merry Christmas!" and were off into the swirling snow.

O'Malley sat a minute to contemplate the situation. He turned up the radio so that the holiday songs filled the building. The jail had miraculously become warmer. He looked into the coffeepot where he saw a puddle of cold, dark, murky coffee. He dumped it out, filled the pot with fresh water and a new filter heaped with coffee. O'Malley said to no one but himself, "What the dickens! We'll have hot coffee, too!" Man-fashion he piled all the cookies into one box and put the fruitcake and boxes of candy under his arm. The Deputy came in the door unexpectedly; sizing up the situation, offered to help.

Reactions from cell to cell were heartwarming. Jimmy, who looked like a young boy, lay on his mattress and was staring at the ceiling. He jumped up and grinned as the Sergeant gave him a choice of treats from the boxes. The inmate's eyes glistened as he took one of the paper napkins and heaped it with cookies. He also took a piece of fruitcake. "Ma used to make this," Jimmy said wistfully.

Stubbs was coming out of a drunken stupor but brightened at the appearance of his keeper. "Got a big pot of coffee brewing," said the jailer. "Save some of the cookies for that. Plenty here...take as you want!" "Thanks...thanks," was the mumbled reply.

A "wino" and his cellmate began stuffing cookies in their mouths and responded with, "Thanks" and "Yah! Man!" The rest of the men had smelled the coffee and heard the commotion in the hallway so were standing by the bars to catch the action.

Patrick, a young inmate, had hoped his girl friend would remember him on Christmas Eve but he had been disappointed. The smell of coffee and the Christmas music gave him a glimmer of hope that revived his spirits. He could not understand the flutter in his heart, "Somebody remembered us," he thought with pleasure. The chocolate-covered cherry tasted like manna from heaven. It reminded him of Christmases past.

An old man in one cell had been fighting sleep but could not resist the temptation and jumped up for his share of goodies. "Gosh, there really is a Santa Claus," he quipped to himself.

Several men were termed 'habituals' and had been in jail many times but this was their first experience of Christmas behind bars. They gulped the steaming coffee and held out their cups for more as they ate fruitcake and cookies with gusto.

91

It was almost midnight when the impromptu party was finished. O'Malley returned to his desk carrying the last cup of coffee. The doorbell rang and three young men asked if they could sing songs for the prisoners. They were dressed in Mid-evil costumes, looking like a picture of carolers depicted on a Christmas card. They stood in the hallway and sang, "Joy to the World" and "Silent Night". Then they were gone.

O'Malley picked up one of the paper napkins and placed a big cutout cookie star in the middle. He noticed the napkin had a picture of the Three Wise Men and the star. He read the printing "Peace on Earth; Goodwill to Men." A big, salty tear ran down his nose and splashed in the middle of the powdered sugar frosting on the cookie. The sugar began to melt. O'Malley's hand trembled a little and he spilled coffee on the edge of the napkins. "What's got into me?" he grunted as he munched the now-soggy Christmas star. He was happy that there was plenty of room in his Inn and thankful for three young wise men for their message in song and for the caring-sharing women who had remembered them with love.

Tomorrow would be a blessed Christmas Day.

Seeing Red from the Apple Tree

Millie Taylor, a renter of 20 years, had been the first occupant in the new Sunny Valley apartments, which were built for senior citizens in the county. It was a landscaped, tri-level, twelve apartment complex which advertised being "near uptown, in the vicinity of churches, fireproof, well lighted, and convenient." Leasing these units was no problem for the local realtor, who supervised the building for an out of state contractor and owner. Many, who were able to dispose of their "humongous" old houses or move in from the farm, were eager to rent these efficiency apartments. Almost as soon as the carpets were laid there was a waiting list of eager renters.

Through the years some left for various reasons and others moved in. The apartments were always filled with middle-aged and elderly tenants who found happiness in these pleasant apartments. They also enjoyed the companionship of each other. They shared recipes, food, magazines, knitting and crocheting patterns, talked about their children and grandchildren, played cards and games.

Millie Taylor had her choice of apartments. She chose the second level (the bottom level was a semi-basement), on the south side which overlooked the front yard and street. Best of all, there was a big apple tree spared by the contractor, which was right outside her wooden deck. From her balcony, she could almost touch its branches. Certainly, she could smell the blossoms in the spring.

The tree was the problem! It had been barren for several years but the promise of apples this year began to mar the serenity of an otherwise congenial group of retirement ladies (eleven in all) and one retired farmer. He was a bachelor named Charles Swenson, who lived in 1A and acted as caretaker for the building. His apartment was below Millie's and the trunk of the tree was in full view, nearly blocking his front window. This did not bother Charles. He was known as "the quiet sort" and did his best to please the harem of ladies who seemed to find plenty for him to do. He was constantly called by one or more women to replace light bulbs, check the furnace or air conditioner, hang a picture and a myriad of other home repair jobs, large and small. Charlie was a man of few words so he did not complain. The grateful ladies were constantly supplying him with samples of homemade cookies, cakes and pies. He also liked to keep busy, so living at Sunny Vale beat the lonesome days on the farm.

As fall approached, there was a ripple of expectation in the complex as the apple tree produced a small crop of decent looking apples. It had been some years since this miracle had happened due to late frosts, fungus or other problems known only to fruit bearing trees. At any rate, this year there were apples hanging on the tree. Each day they looked bigger and more tempting. Millie had decided, using her personal logic, that since the tree was right in front of her window, the fruit below belonged to her. Millie referred to the tree, in casual conversation, as MY tree. She talked of MY apples and MY favorite apple recipes. No one wanted to "pick a quarrel," but each woman had her own private thoughts on the subject. The peace that hovered

94

over Sunny Vale shifted daily as apple picking season approached. The apple tree subject became a touchy subject.

Millie spent hours going through recipes and cookbooks. Her mind envisioned the many things she could make with this succulent fruit. "Charles is a bachelor", she reasoned, "and he wouldn't want any apples."

"At any rate," she said to herself, "I'll give him a piece of apple pie now and then."

The resident above her, Hannah Morgan, also had a good view of the prize. However, she was spending a vacation with her family and would not be home before the anticipated apple harvest.

Actually, by harvest time there were fewer apples on the tree as a windstorm had destroyed some and the lower branches did not seem to have many hanging within reach. Millie thought the paperboy might have picked some while they were still green. She had a plan to enlist Charlie's help. Maybe she could also knock some apples down by standing on her balcony and hitting the branches with a broom. Then, she could pick them up off the ground. Her heart was set on harvesting as much of "her crop" as possible. Then the cooking extravaganza would proceed: apple pie, apple crisp, applesauce cookies, apple bread. It was enough to blow the mind!

Millie reminisced to herself and remembered the big orchard on her childhood farm. Her mother was never without apples. She dried, canned, and stored apples. Millie still recalled her favorite dessert. One tree had big green apples which cooked to a thick mush. The concoction was sweetened with sugar and spiced with cinnamon. Freshly separated country cream was poured over each serving bowl of this applesauce. It was a pleasing dessert, to say the least!

Other trees produced eating apples. Still others "canners."

Unbeknownst to Millie, others in the building were also eyeing the tree and conjuring their own visions of apple butter, apple torte, and apple dumplings. They could also recall the orchards of years gone by. Olive Nelson, down the hall in apartment 2C, had a fairly good view of the crop. She liked to cook and had saved a few Mason canning jars when she broke up the family home to become a city dweller. Maybe, just maybe, she could can a pint or two of applesauce.

Bessie Fickman and Marie Barnes, who lived on the lower level near Charlie, had already decided to enlist this gentleman's service to mount a ladder and pick the rest of the fruit. They talked about it over tea and ginger cookies one late summer afternoon. They declared that since they all paid rent they all equally owned the apple tree. "Yes, the apples are about ready to be picked or the birds will rob us of them," they decided. "Better talk to Charlie soon," Bessie told Marie.

Hattie Carlson, Sarah Schmitt and Clara Bennett, lived on the top level and could see the fast ripening fruit from Sarah's window. They had an "apple talk" over the fresh doughnuts and coffee. They recalled the many delectable apple dishes from the years gone by. They did not think anyone else, except Millie, had thoughts of harvesting the fruit but they still considered it a little forbidden so they decided against involving Charlie in their harvest scheme. They agreed to go down after 10:00 P.M. when everyone would be watching the nighttime news on TV. They would shake the tree and pick up the fallen fruit. No one would be the wiser. Also, it was time to do it! Like excited schoolgirls they met in the hallway at 10:15 P.M. and tiptoed down the stairs, each carrying a handled basket. They grabbed the tree trunk and shook like crazy. A few fell to the ground and they quickly retrieved them. They rattled some other branches and shook again. Many apples gave up and plummeted to the lawn below. The trio scooped them up and ascended the stairs. They divided the loot in Clara's apartment and agreed to keep mum and try the adventure again in a few nights.

All went well until noon the next day when Emma Steele, who always bragged about a keen sense of smell, detected the odor of cooking apples in the kitchen above. She confided her suspicions to Mabel Olsen, her neighbor. They sniffed and smelled in Mabel's kitchen and for sure, they smelled cinnamon and maybe apples.

The following day the senior citizen bus was going to the Empire Shopping Mall and most of the women had signed up to go. But Bessie and Marie had other plans. It would be a good apple-picking day. They knew Margaret Bouregard would be watching soap operas until 2:00 P.M. Then she would take her nap. It was time to act. The two women tapped on Charlie's door shortly after lunch. Bessie explained that her niece was coming for a visit and she loved pie. Marie said that she was expecting company, too, so she needed apples. Would he get a ladder and help them? They noticed a bowl of familiar looking apples on Charlie's table and Bessie remarked, "I see you have some already." "No," Charlie said "my young tenant on the farm brought these to me. I like to munch on apples in the evening. There's a big orchard on my farm but I can't get out there to pick the crop. Maybe my tenant forgot to spray them so the fruit may be wormy. I'll get the ladder from the garage and we'll pick some of the apples in the front yard."

The fun began! Charlie picked and handed apples down to the eager women until each had a small bucket full. Since picking was slim, they decided they had better quit. They promised Charlie some pie for his efforts. The rest of the afternoon the two enjoyed their harvest. Marie peeled and diced apples and boiled them into applesauce. She put some in the fruit drawer of her refrigerator and the rest in a sack of them behind the kitchen wastebasket under the sink.

Bessie got busy making her pie and froze some slices in bags which fit in the freezing compartment of her refrigerator. She wanted enough to "put up" a few jars of sauce but there were not enough left on the tree to dream about that.

When Millie Taylor and the rest came home from the shopping trip, one of the apartment dwellers had invested in a ten-pound bag of sugar. "Sugar? Strange!" thought Millie. "Tomorrow I'll talk to Charlie and we'll harvest MY apple tree." She was tired from the shopping spree but she peeked out of her drapes to admire the ripe apples. She squinted and looked again. No apples! She opened the sliding door and stepped onto her deck and peered closer at the tree. Not an apple to be seen!

"I've been robbed!" she yelled. "Somebody stole all my apples!" She ran downstairs to tell Charlie, who looked dumfounded at her report of a robbery. When he heard it was apples that were taken, he told her to calm down and call the police if she was really robbed. By then, heads were sticking out of apartment doors and women were shaking heads and looking at each other. "Who would do such a vile thing?" they all questioned. Millie was furious! HER apples were gone! Charlie said nothing. All the ladies made various statements such as, "Why would anyone do such a dastardly trick as to steal from a little old lady!"

Early the next morning Charlie called his farm tenant and they had a long telephone conversation. By noon, a pickup truck drove up to Sunny Valley and unloaded twelve gunny sacks of apples—one for each apartment.

The sugar was gone by sundown and Sunny Valley smelled like an applesauce factory. The apartment lights went out one by one right after the 10:00 o'clock news as tired pastry bakers and apple cookers went to bed.

Tranquility and serenity again settled over Sunny Vale. And all could plan to fulfill the prairie proverb: "An apple a day keeps the doctor away!"

NOW AVAILABLE

Signed Copies of
Author's
Ardyce Habeger Samp
Books

Quantity	Description	Price Each	
	When Movies Were a Dime	$9.95	
	Penny Candy Days	$9.95	
	When Coffee Was A Nickel	$9.95	
	Publishers Special (all three books)	$22.95	
	Subtotal		
	S.D. Residents add 6% Sales Tax		
	$4.00 Shipping & Handling		
	Grand Total		

We Accept MasterCard, Visa, Check or Money Orders. Send to:

info@Rushmorehouse.com

RUSHMORE HOUSE PUBLISHING
P.O. Box 1591
Sioux Falls, SD 57101
800-456-1895
605-334-6630 (fax)